ALMOST FATE

KYLIE GILMORE

Cover design by Sweet 'N Spicy Designs

Published by: Extra Fancy Books

ISBN-13: 978-1-942238-68-3

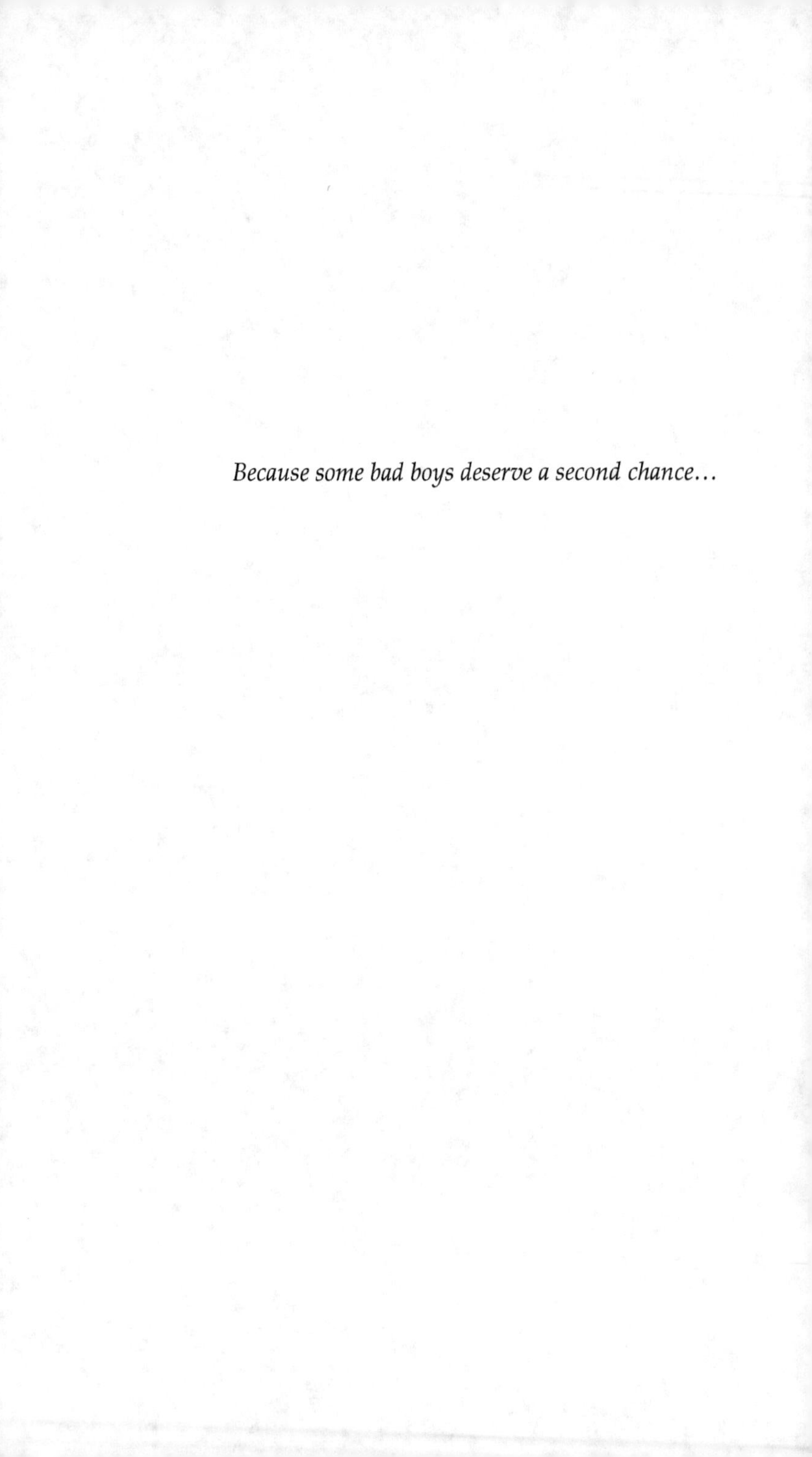

Because some bad boys deserve a second chance…

1

Griffin Huntley woke up with a naked brunette in his bed.

He smiled to himself as he rolled naked out of bed and pulled his acoustic guitar from its case next to the nightstand. There was a time in his life when he would've had no clue who the woman in his bed was—back when he was caught up in the lifestyle. That time was not now.

He plucked out the notes he'd heard in his head upon waking, just a one-line riff with the words "longing for you." He often heard fragments at times like these, just upon waking or drifting off to sleep, and he'd learned to capture them before they faded away.

"Mmm," the one and only "crazy thing" in his life, Christina Olsen, purred.

He paused to hear what she'd say about the start of his new song. She was brash, brutally honest, a real ballbuster, but she'd believed in him from the start. She'd said he belonged in the Rock and Roll Hall of Fame. He still had the text she'd sent him four years ago that grabbed him by the collar and woke him up: *I want to hear your soul music. No matter how long it takes to get your shit together. Hear me?*

Her faith in him had touched him deeply.

Christina went on in her harsh Brooklyn accent, "I wanna hear more." It was music to his ears—the ultimate compliment. She'd say "that blows" if it was a rehash of some of his older work or, worse, "meh," if it was nothing special. Her comments had never steered him wrong even when they were sometimes hard to hear.

He smiled at her over his shoulder and plucked out a few more notes. Her dark brown hair in its choppy short cut stuck out all over the place. She sat up and pressed against his back, her hands sliding over his shoulders before kissing his neck.

"Keep going," she purred.

He played some more. Christina was his muse. He never would've become the international superstar he was today without her and he damn well knew it. When he'd first met her, four years ago, it'd been at a low point in his life. Professionally he'd been on a good run with his band, Twisted Star, but his personal life was a disaster. That all changed with Christina. He'd gone out on his own, leaving his band and all of his staff behind, abandoning the glam LA rock-star lifestyle to move to the hopping music scene in Brooklyn and rediscover what had made him passionate about music in the first place.

He closed his eyes and let his fingers play on the strings as her hot mouth moved from his neck to his shoulder. Desire built in him, but he waited. One thing he'd learned from the year of platonic friendship Christina had put him through before he'd convinced her to take a chance on him—pent-up desire could enhance his music. Everything came out in the music—joy, sadness, anger, love, angst, frustration—as long as he was open to it. They'd been together for three years, and he hoped Christina was ready to take things to the next level.

She kissed her way back up his neck and tugged his earlobe between her sharp teeth.

"Chris," he warned.

"Keep playing," she teased as her tongue ran along the shell of his ear. The woman drove him crazy. He wanted her just as much now as the first time they'd hooked up. Like she was his next breath.

He shifted, held her by the chin, and met her startlingly bright blue eyes. "I'll play you next." Her eyes darkened with desire. Her body was his instrument, and he knew well how to play the full range from soft gasps to full-throated screams.

He set his guitar back in its case before joining her in the bed, sitting next to her. He gazed into her eyes as he cradled her cheek with one hand. "I love you."

"Love you too," she said before climbing into his lap and wrapping her arms and legs around him. She was a petite five foot three to his six-foot frame, and he loved the way she fit against him perfectly. She started kissing his neck, nipping and tasting as she went.

"Have you thought about what I said?" he asked, running his hands down her back. She was never more agreeable than when they were in bed, which was why he brought it up now. He wanted to marry her, settle down, and start a family. His birthday loomed only weeks away, and the closer he got to the big 4-0, the more urgent it felt.

"No," she said, still kissing his neck. "Don't talk about it."

"It's important. I really want—"

"Don't ruin the moment," she said before pressing her lips to his roughly, igniting him. He gripped her hair, taking over the kiss, and let it go. For now.

~

Christina was a lot of things—tough, determined, no-nonsense—but she was not a fool. Most women she knew would've been over the moon to have rocker Griffin Huntley asking them to take things to the next level—marriage, family, kids, the whole shebang. Not her. They had a good thing going, and she knew marriage would ruin everything. She was intimately acquainted with how Griff treated his first wife, Steph, because his ex had married Christina's sweet younger brother (truly a twisted situation and a whole 'nother complicated story). Griff had cheated on Steph for years with A-list movie stars and supermodels; their faces and entwined bodies plastered all over the tabloids. Add in the fact that Christina's first husband left her when he got his mistress pregnant and fuggedaboudit!

She slipped on a little black dress for the New Year's Eve party they were heading to at a friend's penthouse apartment in the city (Manhattan was always called "the city" by anyone who lived around here) and headed to the full-length mirror to check that everything was in order. "Griff, can you zip me?"

He appeared behind her and stroked a warm hand down her spine, causing electric frissons of sensation before slowly zipping her up. He met her eyes in the mirror. She'd never get tired of looking at him. Short-cropped black hair with some spikes on top framed the most gorgeous face she'd ever seen with soulful hazel eyes, straight nose with a cute upturn at the end, permanently scruffy jaw, and full lower lip.

He kissed the tender spot on her neck just below her ear, sending hot shivers through her. "I got you something."

She looked away, fearing he was going to push the issue with a ring. He'd been pushing for a more permanent commitment the closer it got to his birthday. She planned on waiting him out, certain it was just a midlife crisis.

Griff settled a silver necklace with a starburst pendant decorated with pearls and gold balls around her neck. It was funky and modern and perfectly suited her.

"Do you like it?" he asked.

She turned and threw her arms around his neck. "I love it."

He wrapped his arms around her waist, hugging her. She lifted her head, meeting his hazel eyes, and an electric attraction hummed between them. He dipped his head, slowly pressing his lips to hers. She returned the kiss in her usual aggressive way, which amped him up. His mouth turned hungry, devouring her, and she felt her body revving up for more as he palmed her ass and pressed her flush against him.

She tore her mouth away. "Maybe we should bail on the party."

Griff stroked her throat, trailing over her exposed collarbone. "I promised Rob I'd play a few songs tonight." Rob Hillman was the host of the party and star of the movie franchise *Hacker*. The party would be full of celebrities—actors, musicians, professional athletes. "Besides, Ellie from *Savage Release* is going to be there to get an early scoop."

She stiffened. *Savage Release* was the online music magazine catering to the younger demographic that Griff needed to sustain his career. That wasn't the problem. The problem was, as his manager, she'd already arranged the interview for next week and Griff hadn't breathed a word about changing the meeting.

"You mad, babe?" Griff asked, stroking her hair back over her ear.

"I'm just surprised you arranged it without me." She handled all the business end of things for him so he could focus on his music. Until recently, she'd also managed his money, though she was slowly passing that role on to a financial planner she'd hired.

"I thought it'd be good for Ellie to see me in a casual setting. You know, get a more personal look at my life. Instead of just a Q&A sitting at some restaurant."

"That's fine," she said, forcing a level tone. She didn't want to spoil his night.

He looked relieved. That was the thing about Griff. What many didn't realize because of his confident badass rocker swagger—he had a sensitive soul. It was what made his music great, but also what made him tune in to the slightest shift in her tone or mood. She wasn't sensitive at all, but she was compassionate. It was why she'd become an oncology nurse, though she'd happily left that grueling job behind three years ago to work full time as Griff's manager. In any case, she tried to spare his feelings when she could.

He gave her a quick kiss. "How do I look? Did I clean up okay?"

She took in his dark blue button-down shirt and gray dress pants, an unusual outfit for the man who favored T-shirts and jeans. The long sleeves hid his tattoos. He'd changed his ex-wife's name to a decorative spiral motif. He'd wanted to add her name, but Christina never wanted to become a permanent decoration.

"Not bad," she teased.

"Not bad," he growled before pinching her butt. She yelped and smacked his arm away.

He gave her a small smile. "Ready for the crazy?" He meant was she ready to face the crowd that always hovered outside their brownstone. His fans kept close tabs on him.

She nodded, slipped into her heels, and headed downstairs. She punched in the security code by the front door to disable the alarm system while Griff got their coats and then bounced in place, psyching himself up. He didn't have a bodyguard, but she'd insisted on the alarm system when they'd woken up one night at three a.m. to find a naked young woman in their bedroom, watching Griff sleep. So-o-o creepy.

He helped her into her long white wool coat and then pulled on his signature black leather jacket and a gray knit cap.

"Get set," he said with a grin. He loved the spotlight.

She stroked his scruffy jaw. "Go."

Griff went out first, shielding her from the paparazzi with his body. The crowd of mostly women hovering near their waiting limo went wild with screams.

"There he is!"

"It's Griffin Huntley!"

"Griffin! Over here! Over here!"

"I love you, Griffin!"

She locked the door behind them and hit the code. Griff smiled and did a hand wave that took them all in. He stopped to sign a few autographs while she got into the limo. Some paparazzi nearby snapped pictures as Griff smiled the whole time. After a few minutes, he gave his usual apologetic smiling goodbye and joined her in the limo.

They took off, heading into the city. Griff stretched out his arms along the backseat of the limo, resting one hand on her shoulder. "Not as many as I thought," he said.

"It's New Year's Eve," she replied. "I'm sure most people are at parties. And it is thirty degrees out."

He nodded. He lived for the fans as much as they lived for him. If there wasn't a huge crowd, he worried people were forgetting about him. She knew it was good he embraced publicity, but, at the same time, sometimes it went to his head. Her job was to bring him back to earth every once in a while. For the most part, she embraced the fame. After all, she'd helped build it.

Once they arrived at the party, Griff was immediately surrounded by a circle of admirers, and she drifted away in search of a drink. His charisma alone would've kept him the center of attention, but his fame had reached all-new levels after this year's global tour and record-breaking album. Even other celebrities looked at him in awe. It was everything she'd dreamed of for him and she reminded herself of that whenever it was hard to share him.

She snagged a glass of champagne from a tuxedoed waiter moving among the guests, said hello to the few people she recognized, and worked her way back to Griff. He was smiling and chatting with two beautiful blond actresses when his gaze landed on her and his face lit up with a genuine smile that always made her feel better.

He pulled her over to his side. "This is my manager and girlfriend, Christina," he said, introducing her to the two young women as he always did. Sometimes he threw in "ballbuster" or "muse," depending on his mood, always in an affectionate tone. Not that any of his admirers cared about her.

"Nice to meet you," she said.

She got a polite hello from one actress, a lip curl from the other. More people pressed in, trying to get a piece of him. A word, a nod, an autograph, some crazy fans wanted a lock of his hair which she would not allow, the nutjobs. And then the young reporter from *Savage Release,*

Ellie, pushed in, hugging them both, acting like they were best friends though they'd just met. She had orange hair and a nose ring, in odd contrast to her almost conservative long-sleeved navy blue dress with a ruffle on the bottom. Christina was immediately wary. Some of the slicker reporters were like that, acting super friendly to get the stars to let their guard down and give them some personal admission that would become headline news.

Within a few minutes of chitchat about the weather and Griff's latest album, Griff announced he was going to play. He settled with his guitar on a burgundy crushed-velvet sofa in the living room and everyone crowded in to listen. She finished her champagne, set the glass down on a nearby tray, and stood to the right side where he always knew to look for her.

He strummed a few notes, tuning his guitar, and the room fell silent.

He always started with his breakout song, "Crazy Thing," which was based on her. He'd once thought she was crazy when she fought on her brother's behalf to get Griff to divorce his first wife (only so her brother could marry her). He continued with a few of his new rocking anthems and finished with a ballad that she'd heard many, many times about a love that went soul deep. He'd written it not about a woman, but about his passion for music. Another reason she knew better than to marry him—she'd always come in second in his heart. She was much too practical to spend even one minute worrying over it. She knew her place, and what they had worked just fine.

But this time when he finished the last note, he looked right at her and said quietly, "That song is dedicated to Christina, the love of my life." She startled. Griff had never ever called her the love of his life. She knew that honor went to his music.

The room erupted in applause and whistles.

Their gazes locked. And then he set the guitar down, crossed to her, and went down on one knee.

She froze in horror. What was he doing? Was this a publicity stunt? Was that why he'd wanted the reporter from *Savage Release* here?

And then he asked her in front of a room full of people she barely knew, "Will you marry me?"

2

Christina fought back tears. Griff had never used her for publicity before. She'd witnessed him trying to force his ex-wife's hand with this kind of devious tactic, but she'd thought she meant more to him.

People were staring and the room fell into a hushed silence, waiting for her response.

Griff gave her his charming smile. "Well?" He raised his palms and gestured to the crowd to join in, to cheer him on. Like this was all a game. Some catcalls rang out. People started chanting, "Say yes, say yes, say yes." Idiots.

The reporter was snapping pictures. This was a nightmare. She refused to play into his little publicity stunt. How dare he use her like this! She did a head swivel, about to lay into him, when he sprang up and wrapped his arms around her.

The room broke into applause. Probably thinking the embrace was an agreement on her part. "How could you?" she hissed in his ear.

She caught his smile out of the corner of her eye, which only made her madder. He was putting on a show. She tried to pull away, but he scooped her up in his arms and carried her right out the door.

"Put me down," she said through her teeth once they were alone in the hallway.

"Don't be mad," he said. "I love you." He gave her his soulful puppy-eyed look.

"Put me down before I start screaming, which will surely bring Ellie out here and plenty of photos for the gossip mags."

He set her down. "Was it because I didn't have a ring?" He smacked his forehead. "I screwed up the proposal. I should've had a ring. We'll pick one out tomorrow."

She forced a deep breath in and out. "We talked about this. We have a good thing going. Don't ruin it with marriage."

He cradled her cheek with one large hand, and hot tears stung her eyes. "Come on, I'm not ruining it. Marriage would be a new beginning for us. Babe, I'm ready. *Really* ready. I want a family with you."

A pang of longing went through her. She'd always wanted kids. She was crazy about her two-year-old nephew, Michael. But she didn't kid herself that Griff would ever truly be a family man. He'd get bored, and she'd be stuck at home with the kids while he toured with a bunch of groupies throwing themselves at him. He'd stray just like he did to his first wife, and she'd never forgive him.

She pulled away. "That's not us. Our life is the music, the travel, the fans, the press, which is great, but that's not a family life."

"We can make it work," he said with such sincerity that for a moment she almost believed it.

But then the door opened and one of his admirers, the lip-curling, young blond actress, stepped out. "Hey, Griffin," she purred. "We want an encore from you." She grabbed his hand and pulled him back inside.

He gave Christina an apologetic smile over his shoulder. The same one he gave fans whenever he had somewhere else he had to be.

And that was exactly why Griffin Huntley would never settle down and be a family man. He was a sucker for the spotlight. He craved it more than he'd ever crave the mundane routine of having a wife and kids. Christina had done the right thing turning him down.

Griffin pulled Christina into his lap on the limo drive home and nuzzled her neck. "Are you still mad at me?"

"Yes."

"Which part are you mad about?"

She met his eyes, and even in the soft glow of the streetlights he could see the tension in her jaw. She was one tough cookie. "All of it."

"Could you be more specific? I need to know what to apologize for." He stroked her hair back from her face. "Was it not having a ring?"

She blew out a breath. "I don't care about a ring. You used me for publicity."

"I want the world to know how much you mean to me." He really did, and if that meant that Ellie got the scoop, that was fine with him. His young fans would dig him as a family man too. He wanted that so badly. He had no family. His mom had died a couple of years ago, he was an only child, and his dad, also a musician, had always been a wanderer. Last time he'd heard from him was ten years ago when Griffin had put out his first album. "Is that all? I can propose to you at home instead."

She got off his lap. "Griff, we talked about this."

He got a really bad feeling in his gut. "Can you shut the glass, please?" he called to the driver, who closed the divider separating the front of the limo from the back.

Christina's mouth formed a flat line. Another really bad sign. "I don't want to marry you."

He took her hand and kissed the back of her knuckles. "Why not? We love each other."

She shook her head. "I don't think we're made for that. Besides, we're happy now. Why ruin it?"

"I know I screwed up my first marriage, but I'm older now and wiser. I'll do better, I promise. I won't cheat on you."

Christina was silent.

"I haven't been with anyone since I met you. Even when we were just friends for a year. You know I haven't." Not for lack of opportunity either. Women still came on to him on a regular basis. That was just part of the rock-star gig. But Christina was truly all he wanted or needed.

She sighed. "I believe you, it's just…"

I don't trust you. He practically heard the words she wouldn't say out loud. He knew he'd been a total asshole to his first wife, fooling around on her and flaunting it in front of the press, but he wasn't that guy anymore. He could do better.

She looked so forlorn that his chest ached. He gave her hand a gentle squeeze. "Can you take a chance on me? On us?"

She shook her head. "It's not that simple."

"I want a legacy. What's the point of all this money and fame and talent if I have no one to pass it on to?"

She met his eyes with her bright blues. "Your music is your legacy. You don't need me to be your baby factory for that."

"Baby factory! No. Our child would be born out of love."

"And when would you see our child?"

"You could travel with me."

"That's no way to raise a family. On the road."

"Then I'll stop touring. I'll retire."

"No! You are not giving up everything you worked so hard for just for some fantasy life. I refuse to be the reason Griffin Huntley's life went down the drain."

"Dammit, Chris. I love you. Does that mean nothing to you?"

Her blue eyes flashed at him. "It means everything. And so does your music. I want to be there with you every step of the way. We don't need a piece of paper to have that."

He scowled. He couldn't believe the one time he was finally ready to settle down with someone she wouldn't have him. She loved him. Why did she keep denying him? He told her he would do better this time around. He pulled out his cell phone. There was already an article and picture of his proposal on the *Savage Release* website. His proposal was trending on social media. Fans were wondering if the rumors were true that she'd said yes. He went onto his Twitter account and confirmed that he would be marrying Christina.

He held the screen up to her. "I just told the fans the rumors of our marriage were true. Now you have to marry me."

"I think we need a little time apart," she said quietly.

He couldn't breathe for a moment. His chest clutched and he feared he was having a heart attack. "No," he managed. They'd been inseparable for three years now—at home or on the road. She'd never wanted to spend any time apart, and he hadn't wanted that either.

But he didn't keel over because he heard the next part loud and clear.

"I need some time to think about us," she said. "And so do you."

"I don't need to think!" he shouted.

She knocked on the divider. When it opened, she told the driver, "Let me out here."

"Don't do this," he said. Christina never ran away from an argument. She always faced confrontations head-on. He knew what this meant—she was dumping him. He couldn't lose her. "Please."

"I have to."

And then she left him right in the middle of the city. It was the craziest, worst thing that had ever happened to him—from proposal to dumping in one night. He sat there for a moment in shock, unsure what to do. He had nowhere to go, no family, no friends he could trust with the kind of grief that swamped him. But he couldn't go home. Her scent was in the sheets, her clothes in the closet, her toothbrush next to his in the holder. His chest ached. Everything would remind him that she was gone.

"Can you just drive around the city for a few hours?" he asked the driver.

"Yes, sir."

He sank back in his seat and threw his arm over his eyes to hide the stinging tears. After an hour of wallowing, he checked his cell to see if Christina had said anything online about him. Maybe she'd tell everyone she'd said no to his proposal. He scoured all the usual news sites and then went on to the music sites. Nothing from Christina, but a small article caught his eye. Ron Colton, guitar player of the White Lions, dead at the age of sixty-five.

He swallowed hard. That was his dad.

Christina went to her parents' house in Brooklyn, her usual haunt when she was licking her wounds. She had the key and let herself in, quietly stealing upstairs, heading to her old bedroom.

"Christina Marie," her mom called, "is that you?"

Christina froze. She thought she'd been so quiet. "Yeah, it's me, Ma."

"We'll talk in the morning," her mom said. She knew Christina returned home when she needed comfort. She'd spent a good amount of time back home after her divorce.

"Okay." She went to her old twin-size bed with its pink plaid comforter and flopped down. But she couldn't sleep. After a half hour of restless tossing and turning, she quietly grabbed some fresh sheets from the linen closet and made up the bed. Then she took off her dress and slipped under the covers.

She still couldn't sleep. She missed the heat of Griff. She was used to sleeping, skin on skin, pressed up against him. Hot tears stung her eyes. She was beyond exhausted. What was she going to do about Griff? He kept pushing and pushing for something she knew was just going to ruin everything.

He'd been on this kick ever since Thanksgiving at her brother and sister-in-law's house. She got it. He saw their happy little family and thought it'd be cool to have that for himself. But they weren't meant for that. She had too much baggage from her first marriage, and, honestly, she didn't trust him. He'd swear up and down to be faithful, but she knew the temptations of the road would be too much for him to resist. That was the bad part about falling in love with an internationally famous rock star—you couldn't have a normal life.

The tears finally fell in earnest. She cried until she had nothing left and finally fell into an exhausted sleep. When she woke to an empty bed, it was with the dawning realization that she didn't care about having a normal life, she just wanted him.

"What happened?" her mom asked when she got down to the kitchen. She set a plate of scrambled eggs, bacon, and toast in front of Christina. Then a cup of coffee that was half cream and no sugar. Her Italian mom always did know how to feed her.

"Nothing," she said, taking a fortifying sip of coffee. "Just a little fight."

"He running around on you?" her mom asked, narrowing her blue-green eyes. "Men do. They stray. Not your father, of course. The man is still hot for me." She patted her dyed black hair in its short bob. "Whadda ya gonna do?"

Christina cringed. "Ma, please. TMI."

"Was he a cheating, lowlife rat?"

"No." She sipped her coffee.

"Then what's the problem?" her mom asked, settling at the table with her own coffee.

Christina was not about to tell her mom Griff proposed. She'd get excited. Her mom still held out hope for more grandchildren. She took a bite of toast instead.

"I heard he proposed," her mom said casually.

She choked on her toast. "How do you know that?"

"Your brother set up the Googly Alerts so I could keep track of where you are." She smiled proudly. Her mom had only recently gotten a computer. Christina sent a silent deadly message to her brother for hooking their mom up with the Internet.

"Google Alerts," Christina muttered.

Her mom ignored this. "I saw your shocked face. I guess it was a bad shock?"

She sighed. "You know Griff. He belongs to the fans. Not to me."

"Meh. I dunno. Every time I see a picture of him, he's only got eyes for you. And at Thanksgiving, he spent a lot of time with our little Michael." She raised a brow in question.

"A nephew is one thing. His own kids are another." She pushed the eggs around on her plate. "That's not us."

"Kids are overrated," her mom proclaimed, gesturing wildly. "They take and take and take and then they leave you!"

"Ma, we visit." She and her brother, Dave, both lived nearby. She was still in Brooklyn, and Dave and his family were an hour and a half away in the suburbs of Clover Park, Connecticut. The woman knew how to lay on the guilt.

Her mom waved a hand in the air dismissively. "What do I care if I never get a grandbaby out of you? Sure, you're thirty-six years old already, but do I care? No, I do not. Of course your aunt Helen, that's all she can talk about. Her little Sammi, Joey, and Charlie. Pfft. Just a bunch of hassle if you ask me."

"You can't guilt me into giving you grandbabies."

Her mom took her hand and squeezed. "But you want children."

She blinked back tears and nodded.

"And Griffin doesn't?" her mom asked gently.

"No, he does, but…I just can't see how it would work. He's on the road most of the year. I mean, kids need stability. You can't just uproot them and bring them into that lifestyle."

Her mom's dark brows shot up. "What lifestyle?" She

leaned forward and lowered her voice. "Does he do the marijuana?"

She nearly laughed. That was probably the only drug her mom knew about.

"Or the cocaine?" her mom added. "I heard it's big with the rock stars."

She shook her head. "You know he's not like that." She was glad Griff had never gone the drug route, probably because he didn't hit the big time until his thirties when he had his head on straight.

"You know what I think?" her mom asked.

"I'm sure you'll tell me," she said dryly.

"I think you're scared. You're letting the past dictate your future. So what if Anthony impregnated his receptionist? Ancient history."

Christina cringed. That was her ex.

Her mom leaned close. "I heard they're getting a divorce. Serves him right. You were too good for him." Her mom took a sip of coffee and studied her over the rim of her cup. "Steph's pregnant again." That was her sister-in-law.

"Oh, good," Christina said, the words barely making it past the lump in her throat. She took a sip of coffee. "Good for them. I'm happy to hear it."

Her mom took Christina's hand and pressed the back of it to her soft cheek. "I want you to be happy. If that's with kids or not, just do what makes you happy. Life's too short. Ya know?"

She nodded, her throat tight. She knew that very well from her previous job on the oncology ward. People taken too soon from their loved ones, their lives cut short before they had a chance to do what they really wanted. She knew what she had to do. She had to go back home, talk this out with Griff, make him understand that she wanted to be with him. Just the two of them, no marriage contract needed. She hoped their time apart, as short and as excruciatingly long as it felt, gave him some perspective. Helped him understand that what truly mattered was that they were together. Hopefully he'd stop asking for more.

"Thanks, Ma. I'm going to head back home."

"So soon? You haven't even seen your father. Stay. Have some brunch with us. It's the least you can do after waking me up in the middle of the night with a heart attack. I thought we were being robbed!"

Christina sighed. "You knew it was me. I'm the only one who comes slinking home at three a.m."

Her mom made her blue-green eyes comically wide. "I was about to get the wooden bat." She kept it under the bed just in case. Christina had offered to have an alarm system put in here, but her mom hadn't trusted it. She thought the police would know her every move.

Christina laughed. "Okay, okay. I'll stay a little longer."

By the time she got home, it was nearly noon. There weren't any lingering fans or paparazzi around the front stoop. That was odd. At least she didn't have to deal with any questions from the press about her supposed marriage.

She punched in the code and burst inside. "Griff!" she hollered. "We need to talk!"

She was met with empty silence. She did a quick inspection. His favorite black leather jacket wasn't in the hall closet. "Griff!" she called.

Maybe he'd slept in. Maybe he was still wearing it after their long night out. Though her faulty logic should have given her pause, instead it merely fueled her panic. She feared she'd pushed him away. He felt things bone-deep, maybe he was hurting enough to take a real break from her. She sprinted up the stairs to their shared bedroom. No Griff. The bed was still made.

She went to the closet. Some of his clothes were missing. Not all of them. That didn't mean all that much. He had the funds to buy a whole new wardrobe wherever he went.

She called his cell and it went to voicemail. "Where are you? Call me."

But he didn't call. Not that day. Not the next. She had no idea where he was, no idea if or when he was coming back. Three days with no replies to her numerous calls and texts made her fear she'd lost him forever. He was done with her.

Where the hell was he? He'd gone off the grid. No tweets, no pictures, no news, nothing. And then, finally, some pictures emerged—Griff with his arm around pop superstar Sydney Roy, Griff smiling with his arm around a beautiful young brunette woman, and, worst of all, Griff playing guitar in a bar, gazing at the same brunette standing in Christina's spot! She always stood on the right, front row, and Griff always gazed at *her* when he played. She looked closer. The brunette had purple streaks in her black hair and piercings all the way up both ears, giving her a punk rock vibe, and she was wearing Griff's black leather jacket! Dammit. Griff didn't share his jacket with just anyone. Even Christina had only worn it a couple of times. The woman must mean something to him. More than just a fan. The pictures were from Eastman, Connecticut.

That was it! This New Yorker was heading to the wilds of Connecticut to claim her man. Nobody messed with Christina Olsen's man and got away with it.

3

Griffin hadn't known where to turn after Christina's devastating announcement that they needed time apart. So after several hours of driving around the city, he'd looked into that article on his father's death. No one had contacted him, but then who would? He had no family that would've made the connection between them. They had different last names. Griffin had legally taken his mom's maiden name when he'd turned eighteen. He hadn't wanted any ties to the man who'd floated in and out of his life, sticking around just long enough to get his mom's hopes up for a reunion (though they'd divorced when Griffin was two) and then leaving again. Griffin had grown up poor, one of the reasons he'd been so driven to make the big time, which made buying his mom a house all that much sweeter. His dad had never sent alimony or child support (said he didn't have the funds), and it had been tough to get by as a kid on his mom's paycheck as a secretary. For all of these reasons, he and his dad hadn't been close. He could never really hate him, though, because his dad had given him the most important thing in his life—music.

When he'd found out the funeral was planned only three days away in Greenport, Connecticut, he'd booked a hotel suite and headed out. He told himself he just wanted to get out of New York because everything reminded him of the woman he loved. But by the time he reached Greenport, he realized it was more than that. He wanted to say goodbye to his dad.

After a weekend holed up at the hotel, drinking too much whiskey and cursing his miserable self for screwing up so royally in his past that Christina wouldn't risk a future with him, Griffin showed up Monday afternoon for the funeral. The funeral home, a historic-looking stone house was nestled in the woods away from the main section of town. A peaceful resting spot, he thought as he stepped inside. There were only a handful of people milling about. He'd worn a black suit with his aviator sunglasses and a black cap pulled low over his eyes, not wanting to draw attention to himself as Griffin the rock star. He spotted a sign with his dad's name by the entrance of a room in the back and headed over. About a dozen people sat scattered through several rows of chairs, facing an open casket at the front.

He stood in the back, waiting. When it seemed everyone who was going to visit the casket had, he went up to say his goodbye. He looked down at the man he resembled so much in looks. His dad's black hair was long and shot through with gray, deep lines had formed around his eyes and mouth, but otherwise he looked the same. It was like seeing himself in twenty-five years. A bone-deep sadness filled him. Not in mourning his dad's passing, only in regret. Because if his dad had been any kind of father, they could've been close, and now it was too late. Maybe they could've toured together or at least jammed together. But his dad was too selfish for that and only cared about himself and where his next gig was. It was time to close this chapter in his life. Griffin vowed right then and there that, given the chance, he would not continue his father's legacy. He would be involved with his kids, share his passion for music with them, spend time with them, no matter the personal sacrifice to his career to do right by them. Because if he didn't, he could end up just like this. With a son who couldn't even work up a single tear, only sadness over what might've been.

He pulled a green plastic guitar pick from his pocket and set it in the casket. It was the first guitar pick his dad had given him along with his first guitar when he was five years old. He'd kept it with him over the years and now he was done. He felt oddly numb considering how most stuff hit him bone deep. It was hard to feel much for a man he didn't really know beyond a handful of memories and a guitar pick.

He turned and walked straight out of the funeral home to the chill of a winter day, the sun poking out from behind the light gray clouds.

"Hey, wait up!" a feminine voice called.

He stilled, working on slapping on a polite smile for what was most likely a fan. He turned. "Yes?"

The young woman with black hair streaked with purple wore a long black coat open over a black dress, small silver hoop earrings along both ears. Punk rock meets hipster. She rushed to his side and frowned. "Why did you put a guitar pick in my dad's casket?"

He jolted. Her dad? He pulled off his sunglasses, sticking them inside his jacket pocket, and studied her face. Her eyes were hazel like his, her nose straight with a small upturn at the end, her bottom lip full. All like him. Like his dad.

"Omigod!" she shrieked. "You're Griffin Huntley! I'm a huge fan! Do you know my dad? He's a musician too. Well, he was a musician." Her face fell and she bit her lip.

"Yeah, I knew him." Figured his dad hadn't mentioned him. Hell, for all he knew, his dad had kids scattered all over the country. He was a wanderer, always had been. Good looking, charming, an easy way with the ladies. But, for Griffin, it wasn't entirely bad news that he might have a half sister. He'd thought with his father's passing that he'd run out of family. But maybe for her, the news wouldn't be as welcome. Maybe she'd like to keep her memories of their dad as just hers.

"Did you ever play with him?" she asked. "He was amazing on the guitar."

"Were you close?"

Tears sprang to her eyes. "Not that close. He didn't stick around much after the divorce." She blinked rapidly, trying unsuccessfully to hold the tears back. "Sorry," she choked out. "I hardly ever cry." She dashed the tears from her eyes with her fist.

"He was a wanderer," he said.

She sniffled. "Yeah, I guess he was. I used to wish…" She clamped her mouth shut. "Too late now."

He decided to risk it. Maybe she'd been through the same wringer of a childhood as he had. "He was my dad too."

She staggered back, her eyes wide. "He, what? He had another family?"

"Laila!" a middle-aged brunette woman called in a brisk, no-nonsense voice. "It's time to drive to the cemetery." *Layla like the Eric Clapton song?*

Laila grabbed his arm. "Drive with us."

Griffin shook his head. "I've had enough of funeral stuff. I didn't know him that well."

"Meet us at my mom's house," she said. "It's in Field-ridge. About an hour from here." She rattled off the address. "We're having a small get-together."

He looked off in the distance. "I don't know if that's a good idea." He wasn't up to a gathering of people he didn't know mourning a man he barely knew.

"Please," she said, grabbing both his hands. "We're family."

The tears that wouldn't come before stung his eyes now. He'd thought she wouldn't want to think of him as family under these circumstances. He was a reminder that their dad was a selfish bastard who left his kids behind.

He pulled his hands from hers and slid his sunglasses back on to hide his shiny eyes. "Yeah. Okay."

Laila Colton stood at her father's gravesite in such a huge muddle of emotions she barely heard the gentle tones of the minister. Her dad had another family. The biggest rock star in the world was her half brother. Griffin wouldn't lie about that. Why would he? There was nothing to gain from the connection. She was a nobody. Her dad had died penniless. It was her mom who'd arranged his funeral in this wealthy town, where he'd had his first big gig. Her mom hoped to preserve his legacy, though they'd divorced long ago.

Anger and overwhelming sadness swamped her over her dad's passing. She'd hated him for leaving them. He'd been the buffer between her and her mother, an extremely strict woman who sucked all the joy out of any occasion. Her dad had explained to her, just before he left them, that he'd stuck around as long as he had because of her, but she was old enough now to handle things. She'd been ten.

But she couldn't ever completely turn her back on her dad. He popped in and out of her life over the years—always unannounced—his visits a huge, happy surprise that her mom did not appreciate. Her dad gave her a guitar when she was five years old, the age he said was prime for learning music, and had always followed up with her guitar playing. Music became her secret passion, one she did in the privacy of her bedroom because her mom couldn't stand the reminder of her dad. She had a good ear for it, a good voice when she was alone, but powerful stage fright made her voice choked and horribly flat whenever she'd attempted to perform. At one point, she'd dreamed of being a songwriter, had even wanted to go to college to study music, but her mom put a stop to all that nonsense. She refused to pay tuition for a career as unstable as being a musician.

So Laila had quietly settled in as a waitress at Ernie's Diner in Eastman, working the flexible shifts to pay the bills on her small one-bedroom apartment and freeing herself to continue her songwriting. But she'd never broken out, never even left her hometown of Fieldridge. Some part of her expected never to make it. Her mom always said it was a one-in-a-million chance and Laila was no better than thousands of other people out there with the same talent. And once she'd seen Fieldridge's own Sydney Roy make it big on the music scene, Laila put away her guitar. Because when she'd seen the star power that radiated out of Sydney onstage, Laila knew the spotlight would never shine for her. She didn't have that special charisma that drew people in. She had competence and a passion for music, but she was missing "it." That thing that stood between great and superstar.

The short service ended. Both her and her mom were dry-eyed. Laila had cried herself out over the past three days. She'd overheard her mom quietly sobbing in the privacy of her room the first day they'd heard the news.

"So sorry for your loss," the minister said, taking them both in.

"Thank you," her mom said briskly.

Laila could only nod. Her mom turned and headed to her white Mercedes. Laila hurried to catch up. She waited until they were back on the road to Fieldridge before announcing, "I invited a guest back to the house."

"Who?" Her mom peered in the rearview mirror, making sure the small funeral procession was following them. The people weren't relatives, but rather musicians that had played with her dad over the years. She didn't know any of them.

"Griffin Huntley."

"Be serious."

"I am serious."

"Since when do you know Griffin Huntley? Did Sydney invite him? I didn't think you two were on good terms."

They weren't. Laila had acquaintances mostly, her close friends having moved on to other towns for careers or relationships. She was well used to her own company, being an only child to a lawyer mom who put in long hours at her job in the city. She had her grandmother with her until she was twelve. Then her grandmother died.

She ground her teeth. Her mom just assumed because Sydney was so famous that she was the only one who could possibly know Griffin Huntley. That irked her enough to say, "I met Griffin at the funeral home. He's dad's other kid."

"I see."

"I see? That's all you have to say? Dad had another family, I have a famous half brother, and all you can say is I see?"

Her mom let out a harsh breath. "What do you want me to say? It's news to me but also not a big surprise. Your dad could have multiple kids. He certainly had multiple women. I fell for it once and I'm smart. Imagine what that charm could do on a lesser mind."

"Imagine," Laila said dryly.

"Watch your tone," her mom snapped.

They drove the rest of the way in silence, but that wasn't unusual for them. Her mom had made no secret of the fact that Laila was a disappointment to her. She'd never believed in Laila's dream of becoming a songwriter and had pushed her for years to go to college and get a real job. Now that Laila was twenty-nine, her mom had given up on the college idea.

Fieldridge soon came into view, a small town dotted with horse farms and clusters of homes. She'd grown up in an older ranch home at the base of a hill with elegant mansions perched at the top of the hill. She used to fantasize her dad would one day swoop in as a superstar and they'd all live in one of those glorious mansions up on high. She didn't dream of impossible things anymore.

When they pulled into the driveway, Griffin was already there, leaning casually against a black Hummer, wearing those aviator shades and a black leather jacket, his legs crossed at the ankles, looking every bit the internationally famous rock star that he was. She found herself smiling.

"Doesn't he look full of himself," her mom muttered.

"Be nice," Laila said. "Please. He lost his dad today too."

"You deal with him," her mom said. "I'll be polite. Don't ask more from me than that."

Like she ever could get more from her mom than that. Laila rushed over to where Griffin stood. "This is my mom, Lisa Hughes. Mom, Griffin Huntley." Her mom had kept her maiden name.

Griffin flashed a smile and shook her mom's hand. "Nice to meet you, Lisa."

"You too," her mom said stiffly. "Please come in."

They followed her inside. She and her mom spent the next hour politely accepting condolences while they picked at the food Laila had ordered from a nearby Italian restaurant. Griffin remained separate, standing alone in a corner, still wearing his black leather jacket and shades. The musicians in the room went to him to talk. Finally, everyone left and her mom retreated to her bedroom, leaving her and Griffin alone.

"Want some coffee?" she asked Griffin.

"Sure."

"You can take off your jacket, you know."

One corner of his mouth lifted. "Make myself at home, huh?"

"Sure."

He took off the shades, sliding them into the inside pocket of his jacket, then took off the leather jacket and black suit jacket under it. She took them from him and hung them on the coat rack by the door. "Follow me," she said, heading to the kitchen.

She went into her mom's small but spotless kitchen and headed to the coffeemaker that still had half of a carafe full of coffee. She filled a couple of white mugs and joined Griffin in the breakfast nook with its wraparound bench. She couldn't help but stare. Not only because the most famous rock star in the world was sitting right across from her, it was the uncanny resemblance to her dad. Same black hair, though Griffin's was short with some spikes on top, same hazel eyes, nose with the upturn, defined cheekbones, the full lower lip, even the five o'clock shadow on his jaw. If she squinted, it would be like sitting with her dad again. Her throat got tight, and she took a sip of coffee to loosen it up.

"Thanks," Griffin said, taking a sip of coffee. He set it down and studied her face. Probably noticing the way she took after their dad too. She had the same hazel eyes, nose, and lips; the rest was from her mom's side. "You okay with having a half brother?"

"I'm beyond okay." For some people the shock of having a dad with a secret family might have been devastating, for her it was pure relief. Finally someone she could share what it was like to have the charismatic talented Ron Colton grace you with his presence and then rip it away. Maybe Griffin would be someone who stuck around.

He grinned. "Is it because I'm kind of a name or because you actually want a brother?"

"*Kind* of a name?"

He chuckled. "Really, though, you can be honest. Hell, I don't care if you're just into the name. I'm glad to have family."

She wrapped her fingers around her mug, warming them. "It's amazing because I'm a fan. But I'm glad to have family too. It's just me and my mom."

He unbuttoned the top button of his white dress shirt and the cuffs, rolling them up. His forearms were covered in tattoos. Her brother was so badass. She still couldn't believe she had a brother. "It was just me and my mom for a long time too," he said. "You think there's more of us lonely only children left by Ron Colton?"

She swallowed hard. "You were lonely?" She couldn't

believe someone as famous as Griffin Huntley ever felt that way. How could someone that had "it" in spades ever feel one moment of unhappiness?

He took a sip of coffee. "Dad left when I was two. My mom worked a lot and we still couldn't pay the bills. Never knew when the electricity or phone would suddenly get shut off. I spent a lot of time home alone, just me and my guitar."

"Me too," she said quietly.

He nodded slowly. "So at least he gave you that. You any good?"

She shook her head. "Not as good as you. I haven't played in years."

"Why not?"

She lifted one shoulder, not wanting to admit she didn't have what it took. That stage fright stole her voice and made it horribly off-key. Her throat practically closed the few times she'd tried.

"You look like him," she said.

"Yeah, lucky me. Reminded my mom all the time of the jerk who left without child support."

"He didn't have a lot of money," she said, immediately coming to his defense. Plus she realized he must've been using his money to help raise her while Griffin was a kid. He was eleven years older than her. She knew that much from reading about him in magazines. She raised her palms. "Well, at least now you know where some of the money went. Me. Until he left us too."

Griffin shook his head and took a sip of coffee. "How old were you when he left?"

"Ten."

"Did he visit?"

"Yeah, off and on. Always a surprise visit."

Griffin snorted. "That sounds like him. Do they know what he died from?"

"His heart gave out. He didn't have a very healthy lifestyle on the road. Mostly just ate from greasy diners and fast-food places."

They sat for a moment in silence.

"You think you'll stick around town for a bit?" she asked, hoping to show him off.

He met her eyes. "You want me to?"

"Of course I do."

"All right. You got any bars around here? I could use a drink."

"Yeah. We'll go there after dinner. I can take you to the diner where I work for dinner; then we'll head to McGinty's. They have a great drink menu."

A small smile played over his lips. "You want to show me off."

A rare blush burned her cheeks. "Am I that transparent?"

"Nah. Everyone does. It's fine. I'll bring my guitar and play a few songs."

"You don't mind?"

He leaned back and stretched his arms out along the back of the bench seat. "Nothing feels better than playing for an audience. Except creating a new song. That's pure euphoria."

It was euphoria to create. And she realized she'd missed it. "I know what you mean."

"Yeah? You write songs too?"

She tucked a lock of hair behind her ear and nodded. "Nothing like yours."

"Come on. You're Ron Colton's daughter. I want to hear it."

She shook her head. "I'm out of practice."

"It's part of you just like it's part of me. He taught you guitar, right?"

"Yeah. He gave me my first one when I was five."

He gave her a knowing look. "Same here. I'll bet you've got that same soul-deep connection to the music. I lost that for a while with the lifestyle, but Chris…" He trailed off, then finally cleared his throat. "But then I found it again." He tapped the table. "We should play together. A fitting tribute to our dad."

"I'm not as good as you," she protested.

He stood and pulled her out of her seat. "No excuses. You have to play me at least one song before you can show me off."

And that was how Laila found herself back at her apartment with the most famous rock star in the world. She let him in to her place on the first floor of a light blue wood-sided house that had been converted to apartments. She glanced at him as he took in her modest living room with its mismatched furniture and décor, mostly flea market finds. A bright abstract painting hung over a pink upholstered sofa from the '60s with an assortment of colorful throw pillows. A small leather ottoman that doubled as a coffee table sat in front of the sofa on a red and orange fringed area rug over old hardwood floors. She had a wooden stool that served as an end table and a black metal chair with a blue cushion embroidered with cute flowers for additional seating.

She waved toward the sofa. "So, uh, make yourself comfortable. I'll get my guitar." She'd stashed it in the back of her bedroom closet.

He grinned. "On the pink sofa?"

"You can take the chair if you want." Maybe he was too badass for a pink sofa.

"The flower chair?" he asked in a teasing voice.

She huffed. "Sorry I don't have manly furniture."

He crossed to her and gave her hair a tug. "It's cool. Very bohemian."

"Oh. Thank you."

"I'll take the pink sofa," he said and settled there with his guitar. She quickly looked away, not wanting to laugh at the odd picture he made, all cool rocker with his black, spiky hair and tattoos against pink cushions.

She headed into her bedroom, done in the same colorful flea market style, and grabbed her guitar from the closet. She set the case on her fuchsia bedspread, opened it, and gazed at the glossy golden wood of her beloved Martin guitar, somewhere between terrified and elated. She could hear Griffin tuning his guitar.

She stroked the wood as memories of her dad flooded her. His deep, melodic voice encouraging her, praising her ear, adding his voice to hers. Those magical times when it was just the two of them lost in the music. She closed her eyes as a tear escaped.

Griffin began to play. The song jolted her into movement and she rushed back to the living room. It was Van Morrison's "Brown Eyed Girl." The first song her dad had taught her. Though he changed the lyrics to say "my green-eyed girl" because her eyes were green with gold flecks. It worked better than "hazel."

He stopped playing. "I take it you know this one the same way I do."

She nodded.

"Well, play along, then." He just sat there, waiting.

What else could she do? She fetched her guitar, sat on the sofa next to him, and tuned it. He nodded once and started the song again. She joined in, her voice whisper soft, her fingers familiar with the simple chords. As soon as the song ended, Griffin started another song she knew from her dad, and then another, and it became apparent Ron Colton had taught his children the same repertoire of simple but catchy tunes. Griffin lost her on the last one, though, a fast tempo Irish folk song, "Whiskey in the Jar." Their dad had Irish roots.

"I'm out of practice," she said when he finished the song on his own.

"Let me hear one of yours," Griffin said.

She swallowed hard.

"Please," he said. "I really want to hear it."

She began to play, looking down at her guitar, and kept her voice low and quiet. The song, "Jarring Halt," was deeply personal and technically difficult for her to play. She stopped after the first verse, her fingers still on the strings.

"Yeah, yeah, keep going," he urged. "You've got something there."

She took a deep breath and kept going. Only this time, buoyed by his praise, she let go, letting the music flow through her, awakening her long-buried heart and soul. She finished in a rush of happy tears.

Griffin took it in stride, merely nodding in his knowing way. "That's the real shit right there. Keep going. I think you've got more to say."

Then he joined her with his guitar, keeping up with her on songs she'd created, their voices blending in harmony on some of the repeating choruses. Her voice was surprisingly steady, lifted by her brother's. It was a last parting gift from the father she'd always loved despite his faults. Griffin, and through him, her dad, brought her back to the music. It was euphoric.

4

Griffin thought it was really cool to have a sister with the gift of music. It was like his dad lived on, but in a better way. Laila had a brittle hardness about her, no surprise given what he knew about being a lonely only child of Ron Colton, but when she played that guitar, it opened up something beautiful that he knew was her soul shining through. Nothing was more powerful than the music of your soul. Just ask the millions of fans that bought his last album.

Laila emerged from her bedroom in a new outfit for their night out—a white sheer shirt that displayed her cleavage and her bright pink bra, jean shorts, black fishnet stockings with holes, and high heeled black boots.

Griffin cleared his throat. "Err…are you really going out like…that?" he asked, shocking himself with his fuddy-duddy dad-like vibe.

"Like what?"

"You need a sweater."

"I'll wear a coat."

He took off his black leather jacket and settled it

around her shoulders. It covered her nicely from neck to upper thigh. "There. Now you look more rock 'n roll."

She smiled. "Yeah? I've been thinking about getting a tattoo."

"If you do, make it mean something."

"So all yours have meaning?"

"Yup. First wife, first recording contract, first million records sold. Lotta firsts."

Laila frowned. "I haven't had any cool firsts like that."

"So then wait until you do. Ready?"

She pouted for a moment then seemed to rally. "Don't you need a coat?"

"I'll be fine. Just a short walk from the heated car to the next heated place, right?"

"I guess. Can I drive your Hummer?"

"Sure."

He scooped up his guitar case and followed her out the door. It was friggin' cold out, but no way was he taking his jacket back. He quickly unlocked the Hummer and got in the passenger side. Laila hopped into the driver's seat and made the short drive to Ernie's Diner in nearby Eastman.

She parked and quickly got out of the car, gesturing excitedly to him. "Come on!"

He opened the door and leaned out. "Should I bring my guitar?"

"Save it for the bar."

"All right." He caught up with her as she went to the front entrance and held the door for her.

The diner had a front hostess stand, a long sit-down counter in back, and a slew of red vinyl cushioned booths with white laminate tables on either side. Several young waiters and waitresses hustled between tables along with an older woman with her hair in a bun, wearing a pink button-down shirt with matching cardigan sweater and a long, flowery skirt. Maybe he could find out where she got that nice modest outfit and buy one for his sister. He chuckled to himself over his overprotective brotherly instinct. He was really digging feeling like he had family.

A hushed silence fell over the place as, one by one, the customers noticed him.

He raised a hand in greeting. Laila stood by his side, beaming. The older woman hustled over to them. Griffin waited for her to ask for his autograph or picture, but instead she only looked at his sister. "What are you doing here on your night off, hon? You should take it easy after the funeral."

"I'm here for dinner with my brother, Griffin Huntley," Laila announced a little louder than was necessary. A buzz of whispered chatter spread throughout the diner.

"You have a brother?" the older woman asked.

"Nice to meet you," Griffin said.

"Oh, this is my boss, Carol," Laila said, making the introduction. She looked around.

Carol squinted at Griffin. "You do resemble Laila a bit around the eyes." She didn't seem to know who he was. A strange experience for him.

"He's a *very* famous rock star," Laila put in. "We have the same dad."

Carol patted Laila's arm. "I'm so sorry for your loss."

"Thanks. Can you take a picture of us?" She handed over her cell.

Carol dutifully snapped a picture. Laila looked at it with a big smile.

"All right," Carol said, waving them in. "Don't just stand there, take a seat."

And with that she left. So much for the star treatment. He took a seat across from Laila in a booth near the front window. A few customers looked over at them, but no one approached.

"Send me that picture," he told her. He gave her his cell phone number, and she texted it to him. He turned on his phone for the first time in days. He had a bunch of voice-mails, texts, and emails that he ignored. That reporter, Ellie, had been hounding him. He just knew she was going to follow up on his botched proposal to Christina, and he wasn't ready to go there. He tweeted the picture of him and Laila to his fans with the caption, "At long last."

He liked to be mysterious in his social media. It created more of a buzz. Laila's fingers flew over her cell phone, probably getting the word out about him. A few minutes later, Carol arrived to take their order.

After they'd ordered, Laila asked Carol, "Could you tell Rick and Sydney that Griffin Huntley is in town and to meet us at McGinty's tonight?" She turned to Griffin. "Rick is Carol's grandson. You probably know his wife, Sydney Roy."

Carol pursed her lips. "I didn't think you were all that friendly with them. What're you up to?"

Laila huffed. "I just think the biggest pop star in the world might like to meet my brother, the biggest rock star in the world."

"I know her," Griffin said. "She's local?"

Carol nodded. "They have a few homes, but Fieldridge is where they like best."

Griffin drummed his fingers on the table, psyched to jam with musicians he respected. "Cool. Yeah, I've heard some of her stuff with Rick too. I'd love to play a bit with them."

"Sydney doesn't like to put on a show at home unless it's for an official event," Carol said. "I'll give Rick a call. Can't promise anything, though."

She left. Laila's eyes narrowed. "What's a girl got to do to get any love from the golden one?"

"You don't like Sydney?" Griffin asked. "She seemed sweet the few times I met her."

Laila waved that away. "That's her public persona. She's really snarky and I can't wait to see her face when she finds out I'm your sister."

"Jealousy gives you wrinkles," he said, quoting Christina. Any time he got a little worked up that some other musician was getting better press than him or more concert dates, she'd lay that little gem on him. She knew he was a little vain about his face. He tried never to frown and wore a special moisturizing cream with hidden sunscreen in it to preserve his skin. No one idolized an aging rocker. They might respect them, but they'd always question when he was going to retire. He had no intention of retiring anytime soon. He'd only blurted that out to Christina in a desperate attempt to show her how serious he was about settling down. But now that he'd found family, it didn't seem as urgent as it had only a few days ago.

Laila's lower lip stuck out in a pout. "I'm not jealous."

"Tell that to your face."

Her hands immediately flew to her face, feeling for nonexistent wrinkles.

"Gotcha," he said with a wink.

She gave him a small smile. "Can I show you off?"

"I get the feeling I'm small potatoes around here. They're used to Sydney Roy."

"They're just being polite. Come on." She stood and grabbed his arm, dragging him from table to table. Once they got to a table, people gave him the warm reception he was used to with handshakes, pictures, and autographs. Nice little town. Reminded him of Clover Park, where his ex had settled with her family. He and Christina visited regularly because of their two-year-old nephew, Michael. He got a pang, thinking about Christina. She'd left a message on his voicemail, demanding to know where he was, but she still sounded really mad. He wasn't sure what to do about her. Should he drop the whole marriage thing? Maybe she was right and they didn't need a piece of paper. But some part of him wanted to know that she was his forever. They'd gotten stuck in this pattern of him pushing and her pulling away. Maybe he just needed to get off this crazy ride and let it be.

Laila pulled him to the next table, snapping him out of his melancholy thoughts. He'd just enjoy this time away. Maybe Laila was the family he'd been looking for all along. The only family he really needed.

Laila was having the time of her life. Everyone loved her brother, and she felt like a total badass wearing his black leather jacket. He'd even tweeted a picture of the two of them together and it was getting all kinds of attention. She felt like she was finally somebody, and even if it was just from standing in Griffin Huntley's glow, it felt good. He seemed to get her too. Guess blood ties could do that. Clearly they both took after their dad.

After dinner, she sped over to McGinty's. Carol had reported back as they were finishing up their meal that Sydney and her friends—Jade, Amy, and Peyton—would be there along with their husbands. Sydney's tight little clique of friends were eager to meet Griffin.

She stepped into the crowded bar with a sense of satisfaction. It was a Monday night, so this crowd must've been on account of her brother. Word spread fast in a small town. The tables in the small dining area were full, the three pool tables in the back were busy, and the bar, big enough to hold fifty people, only had a few stools open. She spotted Sydney and Rick at the bar, sitting with Jade, Amy, Peyton, and their husbands. She'd been envious of the tight-knit bond of these women in high school. They were almost like sisters, something Laila had always longed for. But now look at her! She had a brother. And not just any brother. The famous—

"Ah! It's Griffin Huntley!" Sydney screamed, hopping off her bar stool.

Griffin threw his head back and laughed. "It's Sydney Roy!"

The two hugged and then Sydney whipped out her cell and took a selfie of the two of them, beaming their super-star smiles into the camera. Sydney was beautiful with glossy straight blond hair, dark blue eyes, and flawless creamy skin. Laila bristled. A crowd formed around Griffin, pushing her further and further away as more people got close, wanting a piece of him. A lump formed in her throat. She'd thought this time would be different, but here she was on the outside of the clique again.

"Laila!" Griffin called. "Where'd she go?" The crowd parted and then there he was—the biggest rock star in the world and her newly found big brother—looking right at her like she mattered.

He crossed to her side. "I just met the one and only Laila Colton," he announced to the crowd before dropping an arm over her shoulders. "My sister. You should hear her play guitar."

She flushed with pride and embarrassment in equal parts.

Sydney cocked her head. "I heard you were related

from Carol, which is shocking, but double whammy, you play too?"

"You think you're the only one who knows music," Laila snapped.

"Wrinkles," Griffin whispered in her ear.

"There's the Laila we know and love," Sydney said, looking to her friends, who nodded knowingly.

"Sorry," Laila mumbled.

Sydney put a hand to her ear. "Say what?"

Laila silently seethed. She knew Sydney was just trying to drag a big old apology out of her. Where was her apology for years of being treated like a second-class citizen? Griffin squeezed her shoulder.

"Old habit," Laila said by way of apology. "Our dad taught us both guitar. I'm not nearly at Griffin's level—"

"She sings like an angel," Griffin said, raising a hand to the sky. "Pure soul music."

Everyone stared at her in shocked silence.

Her cheeks burned, remembering the embarrassing time she'd sung in front of Sydney for their high school's talent show auditions and majorly choked. She'd tried to cover up with a lot of fancy dance moves, but she'd nearly died of humiliation over her own choked, off-key voice.

Rick, Sydney's tall, dark, and muscular husband, moved forward and clapped Griffin on the shoulder. "Hey, man, we'd love to hear you play tonight." He turned to Laila. "You too."

She didn't think she could pull off a performance in front of people she knew, especially not the talented Sydney, Rick, and Griffin. Not only that, she and Sydney had a bit of snippy history due to Laila's secret jealousy of Sydney's stage charisma, and Sydney not liking the way a crush in high school had chosen Laila over her. That, in a nutshell, was the problem with small towns—a history that always smacked you in the face.

"We will," Griffin said, answering for both of them. "But first a drink. It's been a helluva week."

After an hour of sitting in the glow of her brother, Laila actually found herself enjoying being with everyone. She still felt a little on the outside, missing some of the inside jokes, but Griffin's casual inclusion of her in his conversation kept her in the inner circle.

Griffin finished his beer and set the empty bottle on the bar top. He turned to her. "You ready to play?"

She stiffened. It would take a lot more than one dry martini to get her to play in front of the hometown crowd. "They don't want to hear me."

"Sure they do. Anyone would."

"They just want to hear you. Maybe you and Sydney could play."

"I get the feeling Sydney's not the attention hog that I am." He gave her a cheeky grin that had her smiling back.

"I didn't bring my guitar," she said.

"You could play mine. I noticed Dad got us the same one. Only *he* would blow a wad of cash on a Martin guitar for a couple of five-year-olds."

Her throat got tight. She'd known the value of her guitar and had treated it like a treasure her whole life. "I'm not..." She trailed off. *Good enough.* She was nothing compared to him or Sydney or Rick or her dad. She didn't have "it."

"Not what?"

She forced a smile. "Not ready. You go ahead. You're the one everyone's excited about."

His hazel eyes, so like her own, burned into hers. "No one has the music of your soul. Only you can bring that to the world. And *I'm telling you*, it's worth sharing."

She blinked rapidly, touched deeply by his words that showed a belief in her, however unfounded. She didn't have what it took, and she knew it. "You go ahead." She turned to the group sitting nearby, Sydney and friends, and said, "You guys, Griffin needs a little encouragement to get up there and play."

Griffin shot her a look.

Sydney cupped her hands around her mouth to make her voice carry as she chanted, "Griff-in, Griff-in."

Soon the whole room was chanting her brother's name, and Laila took a great deal of pride in that. Griffin stood with a smile and the room broke out in applause. He kissed her cheek, surprising her. "My fans await."

He snagged his guitar and headed to the center of the space. Someone brought over a wooden chair for him. He pulled his guitar from its case and tuned it. The bar fell utterly silent.

She glanced over at Sydney, who smiled. She smiled back and quickly looked away, uncomfortable with the sudden friendliness. The first notes rang out of Griffin's most famous song, "Crazy Thing," when he suddenly stopped, hanging his head. The crowd erupted in whispered conversation. Something was wrong.

Laila rushed over to him. "What's wrong? Is today catching up to you with dad and everything? It's okay. I'll tell them you need a break." He met her eyes, and the pain she saw there made her heart clutch. "What is it?"

He shook his head. "I can't play that one."

"Play 'Up on Top of the World.'" It was a rocking song with a building chorus that she was sure would get the crowd behind him. He needed that.

"Yeah. Okay. Could you stand to the right?" He pointed where he wanted her. "Right there. I just need someone in that spot."

"Okay." The request was strange, but she stood where he wanted her.

"Thanks," he said, and then he launched into the song that soon had everyone on their feet and singing the chorus back and forth with him. He was smiling as he played, and it lifted her spirits up too. She was sure even the great Ron Colton would've been smiling right along with them.

Sydney came over and snapped a few pictures of Griffin playing, looking right at Laila, the two of them smiling. It might just be Laila's only fifteen minutes of fame, but she didn't care, she was having the time of her life.

And she was extremely pleased the next morning to see her and Griffin's picture splashed all over the Internet. People were asking about her online. Wondering who she was and if Griffin was with her. She loved having the secret of being his half sister. He'd promised to spend the day with her and let her show him off if she'd play some more of her songs for him. An even trade. As long as her playing stayed private. For once, everything seemed to be going right in her life.

But first, the show-off.

The next day, she held her brother's arm, wearing his black leather jacket again at his insistence as they strolled down the sidewalk in downtown Eastman where she worked. For some reason he had a problem with her usual outfits and wanted her covered in his oversized jacket. She had a good body, probably her best asset, and wasn't afraid to show it off. It was kinda cute to have him playing the concerned big brother. It was a rare mild winter day and the lingering snow had started to melt. Griffin seemed fine wearing his own gray hoodie as a coat. She made eye contact and smiled at everyone who crossed their path in a happy little bubble of her famous brother's making.

And then her bubble burst when a petite brunette woman with choppy short hair abruptly stopped in front of them, her startlingly blue eyes shooting daggers right at Laila.

"You messed around with the wrong guy," the woman spat in a harsh New Yawk accent, slapping Laila across the face.

The slap triggered every fighting instinct Laila possessed. No one got away with treating her like that. She was Griffin Huntley's sister! She was somebody! She grabbed the woman by the hair, was vaguely aware of her brother yelling something and gesturing, but it was all a blur as she took the smaller woman down to the sidewalk in a rolling tangle of claws and hair pulls and screams.

5

Christina realized her mistake the minute her ass hit the concrete sidewalk. But now that she was in the middle of the fiercest girl fight of her life, there wasn't time to do anything but grapple for the upper hand and try not to get her eyes scratched out. They rolled in front of a diner, and she hoped no one was taking pictures of their fight. Her white wool coat was surely stained beyond repair, but the feel of her own boyfriend's leather jacket slapping against her cheek as the other woman pulled her hair gave her renewed strength. Four freaking days away from a proposal and already a beautiful brunette was wearing his jacket!

Christina launched herself, making them roll closer to the diner's front door as she struggled to get on top of the woman. She'd either die from a door slamming her head or from this nutjob finishing her off. The woman's nails dug into Christina's neck, the stinging stab surely drawing blood. Somehow Christina managed to get on top of the woman and restrained her wrists above her head by putting her full weight on them.

"Get off me, you psycho," the woman spat. Christina was momentarily startled as she met strangely familiar hazel eyes, which gave the woman enough time to get her wrists free and roll out from under her.

The woman stood and glared at her. She had a small pink handprint on her cheek from where Christina had slapped her. In hindsight, she probably should've slapped Griff instead. No word from him for four whole days, ignoring her voicemails, and then popping up in the gossip mags with two beautiful women. She recognized pop superstar Sydney Roy. Sydney was married, but that didn't mean as much in the music world as it did in real life. And *this one.* This sexy young brunette was seen smiling and standing in Christina's spot during an impromptu performance with Christina's man. The head-line from Griff's own tweet said "At long last" like he was reunited with the love of his life. Her rage had built with alarming speed on the drive out here. Of course, her mom's repeated texts asking *who is this gorgeous woman with your Griffin?* hadn't helped.

Her breath was coming hard and her hands were in fists. That black leather jacket on another woman was driving her crazy! She reached out again, grabbing the sleeve to rip it off the woman when strong arms wrapped around her, pulling her away and back on the sidewalk.

Griff's arms pinned Christina's arms to her sides. She was so relieved to be back in his arms that all the fight went out of her. The taller woman stepped onto the side-walk in front of her and continued glaring. Christina gritted her teeth.

"Let her go, Griffin," the brunette woman snarled. "I can take her."

Griff piped up in an oddly cheerful voice. "Laila, I'd

like you to meet Christina, the one and only crazy thing in my life. Christina, meet my half sister, Laila."

A rare blush burned Christina's cheeks. Now who was the idiot? But how was she supposed to know? Griff never mentioned a sister. He always said he had no family. Wait a minute.

She yanked free of Griff's grip and turned to face him. "How do you know she's your sister?"

He smoothed her hair, which was probably sticking up like crazy from that hellion. "She told me."

"She told you? Really?" He couldn't possibly be that naive. Everyone wanted to get close to him because of his fame.

He nodded. "And she knows the same songs I do. From our dad."

"Like what?"

"Brown Eyed Girl."

"Everyone knows that one!" Christina turned and narrowed her eyes at the woman claiming to be related to Griff. "I want to see your birth certificate. Some kind of ID. Maybe a DNA test."

"You *are* crazy," Laila said, pulling Griff's leather jacket back in place over one shoulder.

"You're not spending one more minute with him until you prove who you are!" Christina barked.

Laila pulled her wallet out of her purse and produced a driver's license. "See? Laila Colton. Our dad's Ron Colton."

Christina turned to Griff. "Your dad's Ron Colton? From the White Lions and the Chilies and the Deaf Trombones?"

"Yes," Griff said quietly.

"Why didn't you ever tell me any of this?" Christina asked.

Griff's mouth formed a flat line. "My dad and I weren't close."

Christina stared in shock for a moment. Ron Colton was well known for his talents as a kickass guitar player. In three years, Griff had never mentioned the connection or that he had a half sister. What else wasn't he telling her?

Griff shook his head. "I can't believe you slapped my sister."

"What was I supposed to think?" Christina hollered. "She's wearing your jacket." She turned back to Laila. "She's young and beautiful! She took my spot when you played!" Her eyes stung with an embarrassing rush of tears.

Laila gave her a small smile. "You think I'm beautiful?"

"You're stunning," Christina spat.

Laila turned to Griff. "I like her."

Griff scowled. "Great. Now you can be best friends. Why do the women in my life have to be nuts?"

"Hey!" Christina and Laila said at the same time.

"Sorry I slapped you," Christina said to Laila. "I should've slapped him."

"Hey!" Griff protested.

Christina did a head swivel and advanced on Griff. "Four days I waited to hear from you." She jabbed him in the chest, making him back up. "Four days you ignored my voicemails." Another jab and he backed up against the wall of the diner. "I have to see you with *two* beautiful women. Oh, yes, I saw you with Sydney Roy. And the headlines announcing you're cheating on your girlfriend after proposing. With no word from you! How do you think that makes me feel?"

"You said we were taking a break," Griff said in a level tone that infuriated her.

Laila hissed out a breath.

"I said we needed some time apart to think!" Christina hollered.

"Sorry, babe," Griff said. "My voicemail was full of calls from that *Savage Release* reporter, so I just stopped checking it."

"I know! You blew off your interview this week completely. She's been calling me too. Griff, do you have any idea what you put me through these past four days?"

"Does that mean you want to marry me?" he asked, infuriating her further.

"It means I would like to hear from the man I've been living with for the past three years!" She felt like she was talking to a brick wall. How were they ever supposed to move forward when Griff was stuck in this one marry-me track?

"I've been a little out of it," Griff said.

"A little out of it?" Christina echoed, getting all up in his business, plastered against his front.

"Our dad died," Laila said quietly.

All the anger left her in a whoosh. She turned to Laila. "I'm so sorry. I didn't know." Now she felt extra bad for slapping her. She turned to Griff. "Is that why you're here?"

"Yeah." He looked off in the distance. "I came to say goodbye."

She wrapped her arms around him, and he hugged her back tightly. "I'm so sorry. See, this is why you need to tell me things. Why didn't you call me? You didn't have to go through this alone."

"I thought you were done with me," Griff said hoarsely.

"I'm not," she said over the lump in her throat.

Laila spoke up. "Does this mean you're leaving?"

"We could hang for a while, right, babe?" Griff asked

Christina. "It'd be cool to celebrate my birthday with family."

Christina mentally reviewed Griff's schedule. He had some time off between gigs since they'd planned to spend his birthday at a resort in Mexico. But, what the hell, how often did Griff ever get the chance to spend his birthday with a long-lost sister? She had to admit she did see the resemblance—same hazel eyes, adorable nose, and kissable mouth. Not that she wanted to kiss Laila.

"His birthday is the seventeenth," Christina told Laila. "A little less than two weeks away. Think you can stand us that long?"

Laila's face lit up with a smile. "I'd love it! We could make it a big party. Griff, you want to play? I know everyone in town would love to hear you."

Griff turned to Christina. "What do you think?"

"It's a small venue," Christina replied, looking around the tiny downtown area.

"He could play the Greenport Theater," Laila said. "That's where our dad played his first big gig."

"Let's tie it to a charitable cause," Christina said. "Everything he does gets press, and we don't want word getting out that he's doing free concerts."

"I'll send the proceeds to Horizon Village," Griff said. That was the adult community for people with Down's syndrome where Griff's ex-wife's brother lived. She loved that Griff had a trust established for his ex's brother. It always reminded her no matter how messy relationships got with Griff, he still had his heart in the right place.

"Any hotels in this town?" Christina asked Laila.

"I have a hotel suite about an hour away," Griff said.

"Let me check on a rental in Fieldridge," Laila said. "Sometimes the mansions on the hill are second or third homes for the wealthy and they rent them out when they can't sell."

A few hours later, Christina and Griff were settled into their new rental, a large wood and glass A-frame house perched high on the hill with floor-to-ceiling windows in the front, giving a gorgeous view of the picturesque town. The living room furniture was casual and rustic—two beige sofas, two matching upholstered chairs, and wood end tables—arranged to take advantage of both the view on one side and the huge stone fireplace on an adjacent side.

Griff headed to the kitchen with its dark cherry cabinets and stainless steel appliances and started poking around. His black leather jacket was now—with Christina's helpful reminder—off Laila, who wore her own dark green down coat with faux fur trim on the hood.

Christina thanked Laila for her help and walked her to the door, inviting her to return for dinner.

"I'd love to," Laila said brightly. "I'll bring takeout so you don't have to worry about cooking." Then she narrowed her eyes and whispered fiercely, "And don't think I'll forget that slap," before whirling and making a dramatic exit, the door slamming shut behind her.

Christina smiled to herself. She really liked that girl.

Laila drove back to her apartment still a little rattled from the day's events. She wasn't sure how she felt about Christina. On the one hand, the woman had complimented her. On the other hand, that slap! So outrageous! She hadn't been in a brawl like that since high school.

She pulled up to her street and noticed her mom's white Mercedes parked in her driveway. That was odd.

She didn't usually get home until seven or eight at night. It was only four thirty.

She parked in the street in front of her place and headed for the driveway.

Her mom got out of her car. "Hello," she said in her usual brusque tone. She wore her white down parka, but instead of tailored pants and heels, she had on gray sweatpants and boots.

Laila stopped in front of her. Her mom wasn't wearing makeup either, and her usual perfectly straight brown hair was tangled. "Are you sick?"

"No, I took a day off. I just…needed some time. Can we go inside?"

"Sure." She led the way into her apartment, took off her coat, which wasn't nearly as badass as her brother's —*damn Christina*—and sat on her sofa.

Her mom sat primly in the chair with the embroidered flower cushion. She blinked, shook her head, and pulled her purse onto her lap. "Let's get down to business."

"Business?" Laila echoed.

"Yes. One of your father's musician friends left a box of his things in my care yesterday. Apparently your dad frequently crashed at this guy's apartment and left some things there."

"Where's the box? What was in it?"

Her mom bit her lip. "Pictures, mostly. Some small items from when he and I first met…" Her lower lip wobbled.

Laila crossed to her and gave her a sideways hug. Her mom patted her arm and pulled away. "So it appears he left you some money."

Laila sat down on the sofa with a thunk. "I thought he died penniless."

"That he did. But he took out a life-insurance policy ten

years ago and named you as the sole beneficiary." She pulled a thick envelope from her purse and handed it over. "He left you five hundred thousand."

Laila opened the envelope with a shaking hand, quickly scanning the policy. Whoa. This was enough money for a fresh start anywhere in the world. Enough to buy a house of her own. Decorate it however she wanted, maybe even have a yard with a dog. Her current apartment didn't allow pets.

Her mom went on, dabbing at her eyes with a tissue. "His friend, Mike, said that he wanted to do right by you in death. Even if he had nothing to give you in life."

Tears stung her eyes. If only her dad had understood she just wanted him, not money. She never cared that much about money. Music was her passion. The only thing that ever really mattered to her. And that was all because of him.

Of course, she wouldn't say no to money, either. She was a little too familiar with the end-of-the-month lack of funds before the next paycheck.

"Are you going to give your brother his share?" her mom asked.

Her hand tightened on the papers. "Share?"

"It just seems like the right thing to do. I don't know why he wasn't included, but usually you leave an inheritance to all of your children equally."

"Maybe he knew Griff didn't need the money." Her brother was a superstar.

Her mom stood and pursed her lips. "Well, of course, you need to do what you feel is right."

She left in a hurry, leaving Laila sitting there, her thoughts ping-ponging all over the place. What was the right thing to do? If she told Griffin about the money, would he feel hurt that he'd been left out of the only inheritance their dad had? She sure would. But if she didn't tell him, was she cheating him out of his rightful inheritance? After all, he was the oldest, he should've rightfully inherited *something*.

She didn't know what to do, so she did what she always did in difficult situations—hid it away to be dealt with later.

6

Christina speared another forkful of chicken pot pie. "The food is wonderful. Thanks so much for bringing it."

"You're welcome," Laila murmured from where she sat across the table in the kitchen of their new rental. "It's from the diner where I work."

Something was up with her, Christina thought. She seemed docile and withdrawn all through dinner, not at all the fierce, fiery woman she'd been earlier in the day.

"I'm thinking after the concert, we should have people come back here to party," Griff said after finishing his order of meat loaf, mashed potatoes, and string beans.

"You want to invite everyone from the concert?" Christina asked. "I don't think we can all fit."

"Nah," Griff said. "Just some VIPs. Maybe give my old bandmates a call. Laila, of course."

Laila brightened at this.

"Musician friends only," Griff said. "I want to hang with people who feel the music. Maybe we can get Laila to jam with us on her guitar."

Christina turned to Laila. "I'd love to hear you play."

Laila shook her head. "I'm not any good."

Griff put up a hand. "Don't listen to her, Chris. She's got music in her blood."

Laila blushed furiously and stood abruptly, leaving half her chicken pot pie on the plate. "I should get going. I'll leave you two alone."

"We'll talk," Christina said. "Soon, okay?"

Laila backed out of the room, whirled, and headed out the door. "Bye!"

Christina turned to Griff. "Did she seem different to you?"

He shrugged. "Maybe she's tired. It's only been a day since the funeral."

True. "She any good?"

"Yeah, she's good. She's got an ear, talent, passion. Just no confidence. A musician who doesn't play is one miserable son of a bitch."

"You'll set her straight. Maybe you can get her to join you in a song at the concert."

"Yeah."

She studied him for a moment, a little surprised at how quiet he'd been about his dad passing considering how deeply he felt most things. "How're you doing? You okay after the funeral?"

He blew out a breath. "I'm kinda numb. I don't think it's really hit me yet."

Christina stood and crossed to his side of the table, running her fingers through the silky black hair at the nape of his neck. "I'm here for you."

"I don't want to think about that right now. I just want to be with you." He stood and pulled her close, running his hands from the outside of her legs, over her hips, stopping to rest on her waist. "I love when you wear these thin, tight little pants."

She smiled. "Leggings." She always wore black leggings with her oversized purple sweater.

"Leggings," he repeated and lifted her. She immediately wrapped her arms and legs around him, dinner forgotten. His warm lips grazed against hers as he spoke. "So…is this the part where we have makeup sex?"

"I thought you'd never ask."

She kissed him passionately. He turned so her back was against the wall, continuing their kiss, the hard planes of his body pressing against her. She moaned in the back of her throat.

He lifted his head. "Too many windows here." He headed upstairs, still carrying her plastered to his front. "I missed you, crazy thing," he murmured.

She ran her hands through his silky black hair. "I missed you like crazy."

They got to the master bedroom, a huge king-size bed already made up for them. Griff laid her down on the bed, kicked off his shoes, and slowly climbed on top of her before kissing her long and deep. He was a thorough lover, never in a rush, always savoring their time together. She wrapped her arms around his neck as he settled between her legs. They kissed for a long time before he shifted to kiss her jawline, her throat, up to her ear. She ran her hands down his back and started tugging his T-shirt up.

He spoke in a low tone near her ear. "What did you decide?"

"Hmm…" She slipped her hands under his shirt and over his muscular back, loving the heat and strength of him.

"You said you needed time to think about us." He

stroked her hair back from her face in a tender gesture. "What did you decide?"

She met his soulful hazel eyes. "I decided I want to be with you. I don't care about having a normal life."

"You know what, babe? It's okay. I don't need you to give me family. I've got Laila now." He moved to her neck, and she stiffened. He raised his head. "What's wrong?"

"What do you mean 'I've got Laila now'?"

"I've got family. That's all I need. We don't have to get married, kids, the whole family thing."

"So that's it? You have a sister and now you don't need a wife?"

"What're you getting so mad about? I thought you said we didn't need a piece of paper."

She turned her head away. What was wrong with her? She had said that, and up until this very minute when Griff had let her off the hook, she was sure that them getting married would be a huge mistake. But some part of her felt a huge loss.

She pushed at his chest. "Let me up."

He rolled off her. "I'm confused."

She rolled out of bed and stood. "Me too."

"Should we, uh, talk about it?"

She pressed a hand to her forehead. It was sweet that he wanted to talk it out, but her emotions were in such a tangle she didn't even know what to say. "Maybe later."

He stood and wrapped his arms around her from behind. "You're not going to leave me like this, are you? I'm getting flashbacks to the year of blueballs you put me through when we were just friends."

She couldn't even laugh. She pulled away and made a quick exit. His loud groan of frustration followed her into the hallway.

Griffin tried to think cooling thoughts before he went downstairs for his guitar. Christina was sitting at the kitchen table, her back to him, staring out the back patio door into the night. He couldn't win with her. First she was pulling away because he wanted to marry her, and now she was pulling away because he didn't. It wasn't that he didn't want to anymore, but he didn't feel like it was this urgent thing. Not like he had before when he didn't have a family to pass his legacy on to. Now he had Laila. She was eager to learn and had already picked up a few new riffs he'd taught her.

At least if he was going to have all this pent-up desire and frustration, he could put it to good use. He sat in the quiet living room and played, pouring himself into the music, and somewhere between the dead of night and the first rays of dawn, the finality of his father's death hit him. He played through it, tears streaming down his face, until he had nothing left. He set his guitar back in its case, went upstairs, and fell into an exhausted sleep.

He woke at noon to an empty bed and sat up. "Chris?"

"Downstairs," she called. At least she hadn't left.

"Grabbing a shower," he hollered back.

After his shower, he headed downstairs, where Christina was sitting on the sofa with her cell phone, dressed and looking well rested. That made one of them. He'd slept restlessly, not liking the uncertainty between them and especially not liking them not sleeping together.

"You okay?" she asked.

He nodded. "I worked out some stuff in the music. About my dad."

"Good, that's good."

He headed to the kitchen, hoping for some coffee, and found a pot already made for him.

"Ellie keeps putting out stories that you have another woman on the side," she informed him. "Pretty big news after the party proposal."

"Great," he mumbled. Ellie was the reporter from *Savage Release* he'd been avoiding. He poured himself some coffee, took a fortifying sip, and turned back to the woman he loved. "You set Ellie straight?"

Her lips formed a flat line. "She sent me a picture of you backstage at your Kentucky concert. There's a woman in your lap and you're smiling at her. I had food poisoning that night."

He shook his head. Women were always throwing themselves at him. She knew it didn't mean anything. "Come on. You know me better than that."

"Do I?" she asked in a quiet voice that scared the hell out of him. "I didn't know about your dad, I didn't know you came out here for the funeral, I didn't know about your half sister—"

"I didn't know about her either!"

She stared at her hands gripped together tightly in her lap. "I guess I don't trust you."

He slapped a hand on the counter. "I knew it! I knew you didn't trust me. Three years together and still—"

"I know. It's not just you. It's me and my ex. He ran around on me for years and I turned a blind eye. I don't want to be like that with you. I want to keep my eyes wide open."

He crossed to her. "I want that too. I have nothing to hide. Sometimes women throw themselves at me. But it's not me they want. It's rock-star me. You have the real me."

She snorted. "You're rock star most of the time."

He sat next to her and put a hand on her leg. "Not with you. You get the real me, whether you like it or not."

She didn't say anything.

"So where does that leave us?" he asked.

"I don't know," she said quietly.

He sucked in air. "Will you stick around to find out?"

Christina swallowed visibly. "I'll try."

"Dammit, Chris! That's not good enough."

"What do you want from me?" she cried.

"I want you to love me as much as I love you."

"I do!"

"Then why does it feel like you're about to break up with me?"

She took a deep breath. "Look, we've both been through a lot lately. Let's just...go back to the way things were. Can we do that?"

Griffin narrowed his eyes. "Yeah, we can do that," he said slowly. "Let's go."

She looked up at him, confused. "Go where?"

"Back to the way things were," he said before grabbing her and tossing her over his shoulder.

"Griff!"

"You owe me a screaming orgasm," he said and headed upstairs. Enough of this talking shit. It was time for some hard-core action.

Only Griff had ever gotten Christina to the point of a screaming orgasm. It took everything out of her, left her limp and thoroughly satiated. He'd been extra tender in their lovemaking over the last couple of months while he'd been in family-man mode. Maybe this meant he really was ready to go back to the way things were.

"Okay," she said quietly.

He grunted. Oh, man, she loved when he went all alpha on her.

As soon as they got to the bedroom, he set her back on her feet. They took one look at each other and slammed together. His mouth claimed hers as his hands roamed all over her body. She pulled at his T-shirt and he peeled it off, tossing it to the side. Her heart kicked up a notch at the view—muscular pecs, broad shoulders, arms sculpted with muscle and covered in tattoos. He looked every bit the badass rocker, but with the added bonus of a tender streak. He peeled off her sweater and made short work of the bra.

"So beautiful," he murmured, gazing at her breasts. He always made her feel beautiful, had from the first time they made love, making it easy for her to drop her insecurities about the other women he'd slept with. And, as she'd discovered after their first marathon sex session, his experience was only to her benefit. He'd shown her what her body was capable of, the kinds of ecstasy she'd never in her life experienced before, and heightened the excitement with his varying approaches, sometimes slow and tender with her, sometimes rough and demanding, always with her pleasure at the center of everything he did. He knew when to push her and when to pull back, in tune with her body like no man had ever been before. He played her like his instrument.

He pushed her down on the bed and joined her, lying on his side, kissing her hard, his tongue thrusting inside. He finally let her up for air and kissed his way down her throat to her breast, taking a hard nipple into his mouth and suckling deeply, causing a tightening in her womb.

"Griff," she gasped, "take me." She grabbed him, needing that connection again, needing that closeness. He ignored her grabbing hands and took his time, using his tongue and teeth on her breast, bringing her to a throbbing, aching state before moving to the other breast. Finally he lifted his head and gave her a hot look. She lifted her hips, needing his touch, needing more of him, but he was not a man who could be hurried. He started kissing her neck. She groaned in frustration.

He rose up and nipped her bottom lip. "I love making you crazed, crazy thing," he growled in her ear.

She dug her nails into his back. He pinned her hands to the mattress on either side of her head. "Watch those claws."

"Griff, I want you. I missed you so much."

"You'll have me. But first I need you crazed." He palmed her breast, strumming his calloused finger over the rigid point. "I love to play your body," he said, before he used both hands to strum over her hard nipples.

He played her like his guitar, building her to a crescendo in time to a rhythm that he set. But she was in no mood to be played with. Not after everything they'd been through these past few days.

She grabbed for the button on his jeans. "Get these off."

"First I'm going to get you off," he said, the words a dark promise as he kissed his way down her body. His scruffy jaw scraped against her delicate skin, his hot mouth and tongue soothing and exciting her at the same time. His thumbs hooked under the waistband of her jeans, his fingers running along the inside of them, but not touching her where she needed him most.

She undid her jeans herself and slid them down. Then she peeled off her panties and opened her legs to him in invitation. She was on the pill, so he didn't have to wait. Still he played with her. His fingers trailing lazily down her stomach, inching lower, lower still. She lifted her hips in silent invitation, but then his fingers trailed sideways, avoiding where she throbbed for him, and stroked her inner thigh. She whimpered as his hot mouth kissed along her inner thigh.

He moved his hand suddenly, cupping her sex, making her nearly dizzy with relief. He stroked her lazily, making her moan before his calloused finger strummed her slowly and softly, then quicker and harder, bringing her right to the edge before slowing things down again. She knew when he got like this there was no moving him along. She'd tried everything before from begging to moaning to aggressively biting and grabbing at him. Nothing moved Griff until he wanted to move.

"Please, Griff, please," she begged despite herself.

He gave her a wicked smile, licking his lips.

"Oh, fuck," she muttered before his mouth closed over her hard nub, his tongue playing with her in the rhythm that he set, slow and easy and overwhelming. He slid his hands under her bottom, holding her right where he wanted her as he lapped at her. Before long, she was moving right along with his rhythm, her hips rocking of their own accord as he made her crazy with his lips and tongue and teeth. She tensed as the orgasm snuck up on her suddenly, and then she broke, rocking helplessly against his mouth.

He lifted his head and stroked her lazily with one finger, making her jolt. "That didn't sound crazed enough," he said. "Let's hear you scream."

She trembled in anticipation. He strummed her soft and slow again, bringing all new waves of pleasure to her body all the way down to her toes. And just when she closed her eyes, floating in that wonderfully sweet spot of gentle pleasure, his mouth took over, hot and demanding, sucking her hard. She exploded with a harsh cry. He grunted in approval. Then he flipped her over, banded his arm around her waist and pulled her up, open to him. She rested her cheek on the mattress, light-headed from the quick movement, still lost in sensation.

She heard his jeans hit the floor, and then he was on her. "Brace yourself," he growled in her ear.

She got her forearms under her and raised her head, knowing it would be a wild ride. He positioned himself at her entrance and she waited for his hard thrust. Instead he brought his hand around and started strumming her gently. She moaned loudly. He was *toying* with her. She rocked back onto him, needing him inside her. He strummed a little faster, a little harder, making her breathless, and then finally pressed inside of her, filling her and easing the ache she'd had for so long. He took her hard and deep while she braced herself on her forearms, rocking with his thrusts, her body clenching around him. He sped up, his breath coming harsh near her ear as his hand played her in his complicated rhythm, alternating slow and fast, soft and hard. The sensations built inside her, making her crazed. She needed him to push her over that edge.

"Griff," she cried.

"Give me more," he growled, his fingers pressed against her, just holding her, as he pounded into her.

It was too much. He'd pushed her too far and the sensations held her hostage on the knife edge of release. She shook with need, which was exactly what he'd been waiting for, what he knew was the point of no return for her. He pulled out, and she collapsed to the mattress with a groan because she knew what he'd do to her next. The man had six ways to Sunday to own her G-spot, but his preferred method made her crazed because she was trapped in his hold, unable to rock her hips to move things along.

He rolled her over and moved to a kneeling position between her legs. Then he lifted her right ankle and rested it on his shoulder, pulled her left ankle to his other shoulder, and gave her a slow, sexy smile as he grabbed her by the hips, lifting them and pulling her onto him in one deep thrust, making the backs of her thighs rest against his chest. She whimpered and then he thrust hard, making her gasp as he went even deeper. The deep penetration and internal stroking made her crazed, caught in his hold, as he thrust over and over, pushing her higher and higher. Everything in her coiled and tightened, caught in an overwhelming surge of ever-deepening pleasure. And then his fingers gave her one firm stroke at the same time as he pushed deep, slamming her over the edge, the scream torn from her throat as her body racked with pleasure. He kept going, pumping inside of her as he exploded, the heat and rush taking her deeper and bringing more cries wrenched from her throat in the aftershocks.

A long moment later, he set her ankles off his shoulders and pulled out. She curled up on her side with a soft moan, completely wrung out.

He flopped down next to her. "I love making you scream."

She couldn't speak. He spooned her from behind as he always did and settled the blanket over them.

"New plan," he said, his voice a rumble in her ear. "I'm going to make you scream every night until I own you heart and soul. Until you never have any doubt in your mind that you're mine."

She shivered at that erotic promise, and his arms tightened around her possessively. He was going to wear her out, wear her down.

"You're mine," he repeated in her ear. "And I'm yours. Nothing else matters."

She closed her eyes, too wiped out to argue with him, to explain that it wasn't that simple. Griff, she well knew, had a bulldog persistence. She didn't know if that was good or bad for them. She only knew she was in for it.

7

———

Griffin was nothing if not tenacious. He never would've made it as far as he had in the music industry without the persistence to knock down every door slammed in his face. He'd spent his twenties in dogged pursuit of a recording contract, until he finally hit the big time at thirty. So he figured if his words couldn't knock down Christina's worries over their future, he'd work on her body. She was never more agreeable than when he'd wrung everything out of her in bed. He'd woken her with an orgasm this morning and then went all alpha on her in the shower. No hardship for him. Her screaming orgasms got him off big time and, afterwards, she was open to him in a way she normally wouldn't be with her naturally tough shell. Now she was wrapped in a towel, curled up on his lap, where he sat propped against the headboard.

"You're mine," he said.

"Mmm," she said, resting her head against his chest.

See? So agreeable. Why hadn't he thought of wearing her down this way before?

"I love you," he said.

She sighed. "Me too."

"I want you in my life forever," he said, tilting her chin up to look at him.

She gave him a goofy smile. "Okay."

He kissed her. "Okay." Wow. He was shocked at how easy that was. If he'd known, he would've tried the screaming orgasm method sooner. He'd been extra tender with her the last couple of months because he'd been thinking of starting a family of his own for the first time in his life. He had to remember she still liked to shake things up. A surge of tenderness and love made him kiss her again. And again. And then he was showering her with kisses he was so happy. "So you trust me?"

"I'm working on it," she said gently.

"I trust you."

"I've never cheated on anyone."

The remark stung. He'd never cheated on her. On his ex-wife, yes, but never her. He didn't know what else he could do to prove he was different now. It was so frustrating. He set her off his lap and stood.

"Don't be mad," she said. "I love you."

Somehow that wasn't enough anymore.

He yanked on his clothes and headed downstairs where he'd left his guitar. Some of his most painful moments turned into his biggest hits. He was glad, not because of the money, but because he knew his pain touched others and let them know they weren't alone.

He played, pouring himself into the music, and didn't stop until he realized with a start that the living room was dark. It was past sundown. He'd been vaguely aware Christina went out, though he wasn't sure if she'd come back yet. She could be super quiet during times like these out of respect for his process. He suddenly realized he was hungry and thirsty and exhausted.

"Chris?"

The light turned on and then dimmed. "Right here." She handed him a glass of water, and he drank the whole thing. When he finished, he handed her back the glass and she set it in the kitchen sink before crossing back to him. He put his guitar back in its case and stood, opening his arms to her.

She wrapped her arms around his waist. "That was pure soul. I liked it."

He closed his stinging eyes at the words that meant so much to him. She heard his soul and touched him with her tender acceptance of it.

She pulled away and handed him his black leather jacket. "Time for the real world. We're going to dinner. Laila asked us to stop by the diner tonight."

"She called?" He hadn't heard the phone ring. Chris took care of all outside distractions for him when he was creating music.

"Yeah, I took the call." She pulled on her coat and got her purse. "I'll drive. You just relax."

She laced her fingers with his and walked with him outside. She knew he was feeling strung out, as he always did after a draining day of pouring his heart and soul into the music. He got into the car. Christina started the car and immediately turned off the radio, giving him the quiet he needed. He leaned his head back against the headrest, closed his eyes, and drifted to sleep.

He woke when Christina shook him by the shoulder. They were parked behind the diner. "You up for this?" she asked. "I could ask for a to-go meal."

"No. My sister wants to show me off."

"Maybe she just wants to see you," she said, trying to soften the edges of his reality.

"I don't mind." And he really didn't. He loved the

attention and he loved making people happy just by meeting him.

"You were made for this," she said, stroking his hair. "Made for them."

And she was made for him, he thought. But he kept that to himself because he wasn't up for another emotional round with her over their future. Instead he puffed out his chest. "Time for the magic."

"Woo-hoo!" she hollered, psyching him up.

He smiled and shook his head before climbing out of the Hummer. Christina went ahead of him, held open the door and hollered, "Laila Colton, where you at? Your brother has arrived!"

Laila turned to the door, elated. The diner wasn't overly crowded tonight, it was only a Thursday, but even just a few tables of people to see Laila with her famous brother made her feel vindicated for all the years she'd been passed over as just part of the background.

"Hi," she said with a cheerful wave. "Sit wherever you like." She had to work tonight, but she'd wanted to see him.

Christina chose a booth in the back corner. Griffin said something to her and instead of sitting down like Laila thought he would, he crossed to her and gave her a hug and a kiss on the cheek. "How ya doing?"

She loved his casual familiarity. It was almost worth all the pain she'd gone through with her hardly there dad to have a cool half brother. "I'm doing great now that you're here."

"Sorry Chris took a swing at you. She's crazy in the best possible way, but sometimes...well, you know how women get when they think someone's in their territory."

"So you're pretty serious?" She looked over at Christina, who was sitting there all petite and deceivingly sweet-looking as she studied the menu.

"Yeah. I asked her to marry me, but she turned me down."

Her brows shot up in surprise. "She turned you down?"

"Shh...yeah. The timing wasn't right."

"Wow. Sorry about that."

"All good." He smiled, but it didn't quite reach his eyes. "See you in a bit." He headed to the back of the diner to join Christina.

Laila went back to work, frequently peeking over at them. Christina had him settled with hot rolls within minutes of his dinner order. Griffin moved to sit on the other side of the table next to her, draped an arm over her shoulders, and kissed the top of her head. The love between the two of them was a tangible thing. For a moment, she had a pang of jealousy. She'd just barely gotten a chance to hang out with Griffin and now he was all wrapped up in his girlfriend. But then Griffin gestured for her to join them and, even though she was technically working, she decided to take her break and join them at their table.

"You want to join us for dinner?" Christina asked.

"I only have fifteen minutes," she said.

"Stop by our place tomorrow," Christina said. "We'll have dinner then. And bring your guitar."

Laila jolted. "Oh, I couldn't bring my guitar. You're used to hearing Griffin play. We'll just listen to him."

Christina turned to Griffin. "Did she play for you?"

Griffin smiled. "She sure did."

Christina narrowed her bright blue eyes. "Why do you play for him and not for me? Is it because I slapped you?" She leaned forward and offered her cheek. "Go ahead. Slap me back."

Laila flushed and looked to Griffin for help. Was she really supposed to slap his girlfriend? He grinned.

"What, are you afraid I'll kick your ass again?" Christina taunted.

"You didn't kick my ass!" Laila protested.

"Slap me back, then."

"I'm not going to slap you. You're my brother's girlfriend."

Christina leaned in. "First I'm not close enough to Griff to qualify for a listen and now I'm too close. Which is it?"

Laila tucked a lock of hair behind her ear. "I just...I never play for other people. That was a special occasion. Because Griffin and I had just met and found out we were family."

"We just met too." Christina jabbed a finger at her. "You owe me a listen. One song or I tell everyone in here you have a secret. Small-town peeps love that shit."

Laila flushed guiltily because she did have a secret. She still hadn't told Griffin about their dad's money. But Christina couldn't possibly know that. She probably meant her secret music obsession. Either way, the last thing Laila needed was people pushing and prodding her about her secrets.

"Griffin?" Laila asked.

He raised his palms. "I'm not getting in the middle of this."

And then before she could protest, Christina grabbed Laila's wrist and made her slap her cheek. Not hard, but still. She yanked her wrist back.

Christina grinned. "Now we're even. You play for me. One song. I sense you have soul."

Laila slowly blinked. No one ever looked beyond the package she presented to the world—purple streaks in her hair, funky clothes, and multiple piercings. Her voice came out small. "You think I have soul?"

"I think you do," Christina said in such an authoritative voice that Laila almost believed it.

Griffin reached across the table and squeezed Laila's hand. "I know you do."

And that was how Laila found herself the very next night, guitar in hand, trembling in a near panic as she stepped out of her car and headed for the front door of Griffin's rented home. Her breath came out in a cold puff in the chilly winter night as she pressed the doorbell.

Christina answered the door, took one look at her, and said, "Do you need to slap me again?"

"No! Why would you say that?"

"You look pale and, dare I say, frightened? No one ever died from playing guitar."

That irked Laila. Who did this woman think she was? Had *she* ever played music from the heart that left her exposed and vulnerable?

"What do you know about music?" Laila snapped. "You ever compose an original melody or spend weeks working on the perfect lyrics?"

Christina stepped back and gestured her inside. "You are definitely Griff's family. You'll find me an appreciative audience, so you can get that chip off your shoulder. It's not doing you any favors."

Laila stepped inside and Christina made a big show of flicking an imaginary chip off her shoulder.

Laila narrowed her eyes, still miffed. She set her guitar down next to a beige sofa in the living room. Christina gestured for her coat, so she took it off and handed it to her.

"Hey, sis!" Griffin called. "Come over here and taste this sauce."

She crossed to the modern kitchen, where her brother was rather expertly stirring a marsala sauce around some lightly breaded chicken. "A man who cooks. Wow."

Griffin grinned. "Christina taught me. I find it relaxing." He held the wooden spoon up for her to taste. She took a small taste.

"Really good," Laila said. "What can I do to help?"

"You're our guest, have a seat," Christina said. "Would you like some wine?"

"Sure." Laila was not at all used to being served, but Christina gestured for her to sit down, so she did. A few moments later, Christina handed her a glass of red wine.

"So tell me about you," Christina said. "Anyone special in your life? Boyfriend?"

"No one special," she said, taking a long swallow of wine. She'd never met a guy who stuck around. Lately she'd been feeling like maybe it was her. Maybe she was driving them away. Or maybe she was just attracted to the wrong kind of guy. She was a real sucker for the messed-up bad boy. She always thought she could fix them. And it kinda made her feel good to be the one whose life didn't seem so screwed up by comparison.

"How long you been playing?" Christina asked. "Did your dad get you started young like Griff?"

Laila nodded.

"You must be amazing," Christina said.

"She is," Griffin said.

Laila took a long swallow of wine. "He's just being nice."

Christina cocked her head, studying her. "I got news

for ya. Griff doesn't do anything just to be nice. Who're your influences?"

Laila took another sip of wine, feeling like Christina was trying to trick her into admitting something.

"Big Bird?" Christina asked.

Laila nearly spewed her wine, trying not to laugh.

"Cookie monster?" Christina asked with a smile.

"Elmo!" Griffin chimed in.

They grinned at each other and then at her. "My dad for one," Laila finally said. "Johnny Cash, Oasis, Adele…" She trailed off. She could go on all night.

"She's a storyteller," Christina told Griffin. She turned back to Laila. "It's personal for you. Really personal. It takes courage to put your stuff out there. It's like hey, world, here's my heart, don't stomp on it."

Laila was taken aback. "How do you know if you've never been a musician?"

"I've lived with a musician for three years," she said. "It's his heart and soul, and sometimes it stings if it doesn't get the best reception."

"But everyone loves his stuff!" Laila protested.

"Not true," Griffin said as he pulled some bread from the oven.

"Not everyone," Christina said, matter of factly. "You can't please everyone. He's been lucky to have a following. But critics can be harsh."

"Christina's 'meh' can just about kill me," Griffin said, miming a knife to the heart and nearly collapsing to the floor.

Christina rolled her eyes. "Oh, the drama." She turned to Griffin. "If 'meh' is the worst you hear, consider yourself lucky."

"'That blows' is another doozy," Griffin said.

Christina huffed. "You're not helping. That's only

when you're repeating yourself. And you know when you're repeating yourself. You certainly don't need me to tell you that."

Griffin inclined his head, conceding the point. "Dinner's ready. Get over here, you troublemaker."

"Troublemaker!" Christina exclaimed with a wide grin. She gestured for Laila to follow her into the kitchen.

"You are trouble," Griffin growled before scooping Christina up in his arms and twirling her around. He winked at Laila over Christina's shoulder. Laila felt another pang of jealousy for what they had. She wondered if she'd ever find someone who loved her the way these two loved each other.

Dinner went by way too fast for Laila. Griffin told her all sorts of stories from his time on the road, the venues he played, the people he met. The parties he went to were like a who's who of celebrity elite.

"You think I could ever go to one of those parties?" she asked softly.

"We'll have one right here after the concert," Griffin said. "For my birthday. Get a few people in here. Anyone special you'd like to meet?"

"What about that guy from *Hacker*?" Laila asked.

Christina wrinkled her nose. "Not him. He plays for the other team. You want to meet someone who might actually be interested in you, no?"

Laila couldn't ever remember blushing as much in her life as she did around Christina. The woman was so blunt and in your face. "Forget it," Laila said. "Whoever you invite is fine."

"I'll clean up," Christina announced. "Go tune your guitar, Laila. I'll listen while I load the dishwasher."

"Oh." That had not been at all what Laila had expected. She'd thought she was going to be the embarrassing center of attention while Griffin and Christina stared at her, judging her for her imperfect musical styling. "Okay."

"I'll get mine too," Griffin said.

Laila relaxed considerably. All day she'd felt this incredible pressure to perform and live up to the Griffin Huntley standard, and now it was just some casual playing in the background. She sat on the sofa next to Griffin and they took turns tuning their guitars.

"Play that carriage ride song you got," Griffin said.

She began the melody, her fingers sure on the strings. This was a song she'd played for years. She'd wrote it after she'd watched a romantic movie with a carriage ride through Central Park and felt such longing and, at the same time, an almost toxic bitterness that her life would never be such sweetness. The water ran in the sink as Christina rinsed off the plates.

She began to sing, her voice thready and thin.

"Little louder," Griffin urged at her side.

He probably couldn't hear her over the running water in the kitchen. She took a deep breath and launched into the next line, full volume like she did when she was alone.

"Such sweet tenderness

"Never to be

"Carriage ride by your side

"Not for me

"Snowflakes on your hair

"I don't care

"Never gonna be, never gonna be like that for me…"

She finished to stone-cold silence and looked up almost as if from a trance. Griffin was nodding with a small smile playing over his lips. He looked to Christina, and Laila did too. Christina was standing by the sink, just listening. The faucet was off and Laila had no idea how long it had been like that.

Christina finally spoke. "I wanna hear more."

"Oh, I couldn't," Laila protested. "I don't have any more songs."

"No, Laila, it's good," Griffin said. "That's the highest compliment."

"Do I need to make you slap me again?" Christina threatened.

Griffin laughed. "Don't make her make you slap her again! Wait, did I say that right?"

"Play with her, Griff," Christina said. "You guys are amazing. Damn lucky in the gene pool." She dropped the dish towel on the counter, grabbed a glass of wine, and joined them in the living room, sitting in a chair across from them and tucking one leg under her.

Laila turned to Griffin. "What should we play?"

He leaned over and whispered in her ear, "'Crazy Thing.' It's her song. Starts on the G chord—"

"I know it."

They played the song. Griffin sang his heart out to Christina, who looked deeply moved. When they finished playing, Christina leaped up and hugged them both.

The rest of the night was a blur of music; a high Laila had never experienced before ran through her. To be held in such high esteem from such an appreciative audience made her feel like maybe she did have something worth sharing with the world. Christina eventually fell asleep as it got really late.

"Wait here," Griffin mouthed to Laila before scooping Christina up and carrying her upstairs to bed. It was two a.m.

"I can't believe she won't marry you," Laila said when he returned downstairs. "She's clearly crazy about you."

"I love her like I've never loved anyone. Even myself." He grinned, and she laughed. "Maybe you could play something at the concert with me."

"I don't know," Laila said, stalling. She tucked her guitar back in its case.

"Think about it," Griffin said.

She stood. "I should go."

"You have eight days to rehearse. Christina set it all up." He hugged her. "I believe in you."

She was speechless. No one had ever believed in her musical abilities. Her dad hadn't stuck around long enough to hear when she could finally play decently.

He pulled back and chucked her under the chin. "Okay?"

"I'll think about it," she finally whispered.

"I'll stop by your apartment tomorrow so we can get started rehearsing," he said. "I'll tell Christina we need space to create. She respects that."

What could she say? Turn down the greatest rock star in the world who wanted to perform with *her*? Was she really ready for this? And then, she realized with a start, she was. With her brother at her side, she thought maybe she could conquer her stage fright and put herself out there. She did have something worth sharing with the world. It just took someone believing in her to help her believe in herself.

She nodded once. "See you then." She headed back to her car with a spring in her step despite the late hour.

8
___

Christina was on edge. Ellie, the reporter from *Savage Release*, had shown up in town on Tuesday after the press release about Griff's fundraiser concert. Christina had set up a Q&A in the living room of their rental home, but after Ellie's article on Griff's proposal (and Christina's less-than-enthusiastic response) and her numerous speculative comments about Griff's "other women," Christina kept any further access to Griff limited to his concert on Saturday. Unfortunately, Ellie had cozied up to Laila instead. Christina warned Laila not to say anything about Griff that could be used in the article, and she'd sworn she wouldn't breathe a word, but Christina still didn't like the two of them hanging out.

Of course, it didn't help her nerves that she'd spent much of the past week alone. She was used to the constant hustle of the city and touring. Griff spent nearly the entire day at Laila's apartment in a creative surge Christina knew better than to mess with. When he got into this kind of creative frenzy, greatness was born. So she did what she did best, kept herself busy with organizing and promoting the fundraiser concert. She even got some local press and TV stations involved. It wasn't every day that Griffin Huntley played an intimate venue for a good cause.

Griff was euphoric when he returned to her at night and made good on his promise to wear her out in bed. She couldn't complain about that part. They hadn't had two weeks of nothing planned in so long it almost felt like a normal life. Work by day, play by night. Honestly, she felt closer to him than ever. She was beginning to wonder what she was so worried about. He wasn't her ex. He was so spent with his efforts on her there was no way he could manage to get frisky with anyone else. Of course, the real question was—what would happen if temptation crossed his path when Christina wasn't with him? Would he resist? When she was with him and saw the love shining in his eyes, she knew the answer definitively. But when she wasn't with him, she still had that little niggling of doubt.

Her phone vibrated. Another text from her mom. Christina sighed. She was going to kill her brother for hooking her mom up with texting and the Internet. She was driving her crazy. She glanced at the screen.

You want me to come out and lend a hand with the concert?

She quickly texted back. *No.*

She knew her mom just wanted to meet Sydney Roy. She'd been bugging Christina about an autograph ever since she'd seen the picture of Griff with Sydney.

Christina's phone rang. She picked it up and immediately said, "I got it covered, Ma."

"Are you sure? There's not much time to bring it all together."

"Everything's under control."

"I sure like that Sydney," her mom hinted.

Christina didn't reply. It was uncool to ask for autographs from other famous people. She'd explained that multiple times.

Her silence didn't faze her mom, who went on. "Your father and I were dancing to her new album last night—" she lowered her voice "—and a little more, if you know what I mean."

Christina cringed. "I gotta go."

"Oh? What're you so busy with? I knew you could use an extra set of hands."

"I'm Griff's manager. I've done this kind of work many, many times."

Her mom snorted in a very unbecoming way. "Manager. What man wants to be managed?"

"It's a business thing," Christina said through her teeth. "He does the music; I do the business end."

"And does he listen?"

"Yeah, Ma, he listens."

"Well, don't let it carry over to the personal, Christina Marie."

Christina rolled her eyes and bit back a retort.

"Are you rolling your eyes at me?" her mom demanded.

She sighed. "No, Ma."

"I've been reading about the concert on the Googly Alerts," her mom said. "Sounds like his sister might join him for a song." Christina didn't bother to correct her Google reference. She suspected her mom said it on purpose to irk her.

"That's the plan," Christina said. She wished her mom would set up a Google Alert on her brother so her mom would start bugging him instead. Unfortunately, middle school math teachers didn't make headlines all that often. Just a few times for him that were a whole 'nother crazy story involving Griff, which she would've found comical if her brother's future happiness hadn't been at stake. No one messed with the people Christina loved.

"You sound tired," her mom said. "You sure you don't want me to come out? It's no bother. I could meet Sydney and be home in time for Monday night poker."

Her mom played a mean game of poker with a group of women from the neighborhood and always came back flush with quarters.

"All good here," Christina said in a tone of finality.

"Maybe you could propose to him this time," her mom said out of nowhere.

"I'm hanging up now."

"You are his manager after all. Manage him already!"

"Love you, bye!" She hung up. Her phone vibrated a few moments later with a text. She snatched it up.

I'm just saying. You're not getting any younger.

She really had to change her number.

Laila was seriously having the time of her life. Not only was she creating music with her brother, but she'd really hit it off with Ellie, the music reporter. She was *so* New York. She had shoulder-length orange hair, buzz cut on one side, and a nose ring. They even went shopping together in the city for a new outfit for Laila to wear to the concert. Christina had given her a credit card to charge it on and asked her to pick up a new wool coat for her as well since hers was stained beyond repair from their brief wrestling match.

Laila and Ellie had so much in common—love of music, muscled bad boys, and martinis—and had been going out to McGinty's every night together. Even the nights when Laila had to work, Ellie met up with her after, *and* she paid for all the drinks! (Ellie had an expense account.) They talked about anything and everything. Ellie even said she'd report on Laila's performance too, but Laila had declined. She was nervous enough about performing her song at the concert without worrying about that too. She was only doing it to please her brother. In fact, Laila confided to Ellie over her third fabulous martini the night before the concert that she'd written her song in honor of him and Christina. It was a little secret.

"Because they're so perfect together, you know," Laila said, popping the olive into her mouth. "Shh, don't tell anyone."

"Oh, I know," Ellie said, nodding at the same time. "I saw him propose. They're in deep."

"I know, right?" Laila leaned her head on her hand and stared across the room at a cute guy shooting pool. He had a shaved head, neck tattoo of some kind of bird, and a linebacker body. Nice rear view.

Ellie giggled. "It'll happen sooner or later, right?"

"Absolutely. Griffin said it was just bad timing." She wiggled her fingers at the guy, but his back was still to her and he didn't see. Ellie grabbed her fingers, drawing her attention back to her. Laila slowly blinked. "What?"

"I just had a great idea!" Ellie exclaimed.

Laila beamed. "That's great!"

"The timing would be perfect at the concert after you dedicate your song to them."

"You think so?"

"I know so. Perfect time for a proposal. Want another martini? My treat."

"I wouldn't say no to more olives," Laila replied. They were so tasty.

Ellie ordered her another martini. When it arrived, Ellie

raised her glass and gestured for Laila to do the same. "A toast to Griffin and Christina and their happy ever after."

Laila clinked her glass and sloshed some on her hand. "Oops!" She licked her hand.

"I can't wait to see the perfect proposal," Ellie said. "With perfect timing." She threw her arm around Laila. "All thanks to you!"

"Thank me!" She took a sip of martini because you had to or the toast didn't count. "And then Griffin will be so happy he won't even care about the money."

"What money?"

Laila forced herself to focus on her new bestie, but everything seemed a little fuzzy. "Oops. Shh. It's a secret."

Ellie smiled so big Laila just had to smile back. "My lips are sealed," Ellie declared. "Hey, you should visit me in New York. We'd have a blast in the city."

"To-ta-lly," Laila said, the words coming more slowly now. "I think you're my best friend."

"You're mine, girlie," Ellie chirped. "How much money is it?"

"It's all mine, none for Griffin," Laila said. "From our dad." She lifted her glass and looked to the sky, err, ceiling. "Thanks, Dad! You beautiful jerk!"

They toasted to that. Everything was perfect thanks to Ellie and olives and her.

~

Christina peeked out the front window the day of the concert. The paparazzi had found their rental house. Wouldn't take too much digging once they reached Fieldridge. It was a small town and everyone knew Griff through Laila.

"Griff," she called upstairs, "you've got an audience!"

"Cool!"

She grinned. If anyone was meant for this lifestyle, it was him. He headed downstairs wearing a navy blue T-shirt and faded jeans that molded to his body. Work boots too. So freaking hot.

"Do I look older?" he asked. His birthday was two days away. He was kinda hung up on the number.

"You look hot," she replied, skirting the real question. He looked his age, yes, but he kept in good shape and lived cleanly. He had many, many years ahead of him in the spotlight. She'd make sure of it.

He grinned and crossed to her, banding his arm around her waist and kissing her. There was a commotion outside. Probably the paparazzi snapping pictures. Griff only deepened the kiss, bending her over his arm in what was probably a picture-perfect shot. She would've been mad at his publicity-whore ways, but his kisses were amazing and she couldn't help but revel in it. He let her back up and grinned.

"Show off," she said.

He cradled her cheek and gazed deep into her eyes. "I want the world to know I love you."

She felt that down to her toes. "Me too."

"Ready for the crazy?"

"Let's go."

They headed out the door and the press pushed in, asking questions about his plans and why he was in Fieldridge. Griff made no comment, as she'd instructed, only smiled and waved, saying he'd see them at the concert. The only reporters who got info from him were interviews she'd signed off on. He signed a few autographs from fans who'd shown up with the press, and then gave his apologetic smile, waving goodbye and getting into the Hummer.

He drove this time because he was pumped and loved to drive when he could.

"Nice crowd," he said.

"There'll be more press at the concert," she replied.

"What?" He glanced over at her. "Did you call them?"

"Yeah. I always handle the publicity for you."

"I thought this was going to be an intimate night."

"It will be."

"Does Laila know?"

"I assume so. She's been hanging out with Ellie. I can't wait to get rid of that one."

"Geez, I don't know if Laila will perform now."

"I'll be front row, far right. Tell her where to find me and just focus like she's only playing for me."

"Yeah, okay. I'll tell her."

Griff drummed the steering wheel in a beat that played in his head. Usual preshow jitters. As much as he liked to perform, he still had a nerve-racking preshow anxiety phase that launched him even more powerfully when he channeled that energy into the music.

Once they got to the Greenport Theater, she hustled Griff to the backstage of the theater before peeking out at the audience. It was packed. The press lined up against the back wall, standing room only, though the news station she'd given the exclusive to was sitting front and center, camera rolling, with two additional cameras on the side. Maybe they could add this concert to some bonus footage on a behind-the-music video to promo his next concert tour. It was both for a good cause and involved family. Big-time PR points right there.

She returned backstage, where Laila now stood with Griff. The poor girl was pale, her hands visibly shaking. Her outfit looked amazing—a white, off-the-shoulder peasant blouse paired with black leggings and thigh-high black leather boots. Her black hair with purple streaks fell in soft waves over her shoulders.

"Don't worry," Christina said, grabbing Laila's icy cold hands firmly in hers. "They're here for him. By the time you go on, you'll be so bored backstage you'll be ready. And, by the way, you look very rock 'n roll."

"I don't think I'll ever be ready," Laila said, her voice shaking. "I don't have to go on."

"Of course not," Christina soothed, though she knew Griff would call Laila out on his own. He was damn proud that he had a sister who could join him in the music. He'd been bragging about her all week. Called her his legacy. Christina made him promise not to tell Laila that before the concert. The pressure was too much for a beginning performer. After was soon enough. Maybe it'd be the kick in the pants Laila needed to embrace her musical destiny.

Laila nodded and looked considerably relieved. "You think the outfit's okay?" She pulled the off-the-shoulder ruffle further down her shoulders. "It kind of covers me on top, but Ellie says guys go nuts wondering what's under there. You know, instead of knowing by seeing the boobage on display."

"Absolutely," Christina said. "Very classy, yet sexy. I'd do ya."

They laughed.

"I like the hair too," Christina said. "You were made for this." She hugged her. "I'll be far right, front row if you need a funny face." She wrinkled her nose and pursed her lips to the side.

Laila laughed. "Maybe I'll sit with you."

"Nah," Christina said. "Griff needs you backstage for moral support. Right, Griff?"

"Absolutely," Griff said, raising his fist for a fist bump. Laila fist bumped him back.

Christina rubbed her hands together. "Break a leg," she told Griff, as she always did.

He gathered her in his arms and nuzzled into her neck, breathing her in, as he always did. It was part of his preshow ritual to hold her close for a few moments. He released her and nodded, which was her cue to get the show moving.

She nodded to the theater's manager, Alan, a large bald man waiting in the wings to announce Griff, before slipping back into the theater to take her reserved seat.

A few moments later, Alan stepped out on stage and called for everyone's attention by tapping the mike and making it ring out with horrible feedback. Christina cringed. She was pleased to see the turnout and knew they'd done some good here with the fundraising.

"What a show we got tonight!" Alan proclaimed to wild applause. "I want to thank Laila Colton for setting this up with her very famous rock star brother, Griffin Huntley!" The crowd picked up with more cheers. This guy knew how to play to his audience. "And with your ticket sales and a generous contribution from Griffin, we've raised one hundred thousand dollars for new playground equipment in our sister town Norhaven!" More wild applause.

When Christina had dug into where the Greenport mayor wanted the charity money to go to and the cost, Griff had insisted on keeping ticket prices at an affordable twenty dollars and said he'd contribute whatever the difference was. He'd ended up paying ninety percent of the needed funds out of his own pocket. She dearly loved this man.

Alan pulled a handkerchief from his pocket and mopped at his shiny bald head. "I know you're ready to get started, so without further ado, Griffin Huntley!" He made a quick exit stage right.

Griff ambled on stage and the crowd cheered. Christina found herself smiling at his casual badass swagger. She knew he didn't calm the jitters until he started playing. He picked up his guitar, threw the strap over his shoulder, and approached the mike. He strummed the first notes, sought her out in the audience, gazed right into her eyes and began to sing. She swayed in her seat. It was her song, "Crazy Thing," and she never, ever tired of hearing it.

There she is, my crazy thing. Seeing Christina always centered him, and Griffin lost himself in the glory of performing the music of his heart. The music he would never have dared reach for without Christina's unshakable faith in his abilities. He'd spend the rest of his life earning her trust if he had to. All that mattered was that they were together.

When he got to the chorus, he gestured to the audience to join in. They did, making him smile, as they knew the words and sang at the top of their lungs. He spotted Sydney Roy sitting a few rows back, smiling at him. She'd declined his invitation to join him on stage, saying she'd like to have "the full Griffin Huntley experience" from the audience. Smartass.

It was a stellar audience, and he played nonstop for an hour before he took a break and snagged the bottled water that had been left for him on a nearby stool. He took a long drink of water and smiled at the audience. "You all are a real nice crowd."

The crowd went wild.

He nodded once. "I've got a special surprise for you.

One of your local talents is going to join me up here and it's not Sydney." He gestured to the side of the stage, but Laila didn't come out. He could see her standing there, frozen in place.

He smiled at her encouragingly and pointed to her guitar case a few feet away from her.

She shook her head. And then the reporter, Ellie, appeared behind Laila and shoved her out.

"My sister, Laila Colton!" Griffin announced. He went over and fetched her guitar for her and joined her center stage. Holy crap. He'd never seen such bad stage fright. She stared unblinking at the center camera, stiff and pale. He was afraid she was going to pass out. He pulled the stool over and hustled her onto it before taking his place standing by her side.

"We're just going to tune up," he told the audience. "Give us a minute."

She held the guitar, but made no movement.

"Did you see Christina out there?" he asked her in a quiet voice.

She jerked her head up and locked eyes with Christina, who mimed slapping her. Laila actually smiled. The women in his life were nuts and he loved them like crazy. Laila looked down and began tuning her guitar. He brought the mike down to her level and stood supportively nearby.

"I need Christina on stage," Laila said into the mike.

That was odd. What did she need Christina for?

Christina didn't question it. She leaped out of her seat and joined them, standing in front of Griffin, who set his guitar down and wrapped his arms around her. Laila nodded to her in silent thank you and launched into a ballad with soul. Her voice, soft at first, slowly built in confidence as she sang looking right at him and Christina.

"My heart lives with you

"My soul breathes with you

"No more doubts or walking away

"With you I'm here to stay

"What's a piece of paper, you say

"What's a bridal veil for

"If not to show you forever

"You're my legacy

"You can build me up or destroy me with a single word

"There will never be another

"You are my heart, you are my soul

"Make me complete."

When the song ended, the audience burst into applause. Laila beamed. Griffin gestured for her to stand and take a bow. She did, hamming it up with bows right, left, and center. He gestured behind her for the audience to amp up the noise. Some catcalls and whistles rang out, and a wild stamping echoed through the theater.

Griffin went over and hugged her. "Beautiful, Laila. Nicely done."

"Thank you." She pulled the mike off the stand, looked backstage, nodded and then stopped in front of Christina, saying into the mike, "That was my song for you and Griffin."

"Thank you," Christina said. "It was beautiful."

Laila turned to Griffin. "Do you have the ring?"

Griffin's brows shot up. "What?"

"This is the perfect timing you needed," Laila said, "for your proposal."

The crowd gasped. Christina took a step back, her bright blue eyes wide.

"Chris, wait!" He grabbed her hand, and she yanked her hand out of his grip.

"Don't you dare!" Christina hollered.

"Marry him, Christina!" Laila hollered. "He loves you! You love him. It's perfect!"

Flashes of light went off as the press got close to get the picture that would be plastered all over the Internet within minutes. Another botched proposal. Ellie ran on stage with a small video camera to capture the horrifying event.

"Enjoy your headlines!" Christina spat at him before doing an about-face and rushing off stage.

He looked at his sister in shock. Her return look was equally shocked. Obviously Laila thought that would've worked. She didn't know Christina.

Christina left the theater and drove straight back to their rental, locking herself in their bedroom. Griff could get a ride home with Laila. She couldn't believe the two of them plotting behind her back like that. Worse, Griff had turned their relationship into a publicity event. Again. Would she ever get the real Griff?

Christina heard Griff return when the front door shut with a bang. "Chris! Where are you?" There was a buzz of voices. People must've followed him back home for the after party in honor of his birthday.

She opened the door. "I'm right here but not for long. I'm going home."

Griff sprinted up the stairs. Laila and that damn reporter Ellie followed quickly behind. "Wait," Griff said. "I need to—"

"You seriously expect me to talk to you about us in

front of *her*?" She looked pointedly at Ellie, who merely stared.

"Tell her," Griff said.

Ellie said nothing.

Laila filled in the silence. "That on-stage kinda proposal wasn't Griff's idea. In fact, he had no clue. Ellie convinced me it was a good idea and I thought so too. Griff said the first proposal was just bad timing."

Christina smiled sweetly at Ellie at complete odds with her uber-threatening voice. "You will never get access to Griffin again. No pictures, no interviews, no comment ever. If you publish—"

"It's already online," Ellie said smugly.

Christina did a head swivel and turned to Griff. "You'd better get her out of here *fast*."

Griff stepped between them. "I will. But not before I tell her on the record that Christina and I are together forever, whether or not there's a piece of paper saying so, and…" His voice got choked. He took both of Christina's hands in his and gazed into her eyes with that soulful look that she knew was from his heart. "And I don't deserve her, but I will spend the rest of my life trying to be the man she deserves. She is my heart, my soul, my everything."

"Whoa," Laila whispered, "just like my song." Then she turned to Ellie. "You should leave now."

"Tell him about the money, Laila," Ellie said, "from your daddy who loves you more."

Laila gasped.

Griff turned to Laila. "Dad had money?"

"Nuh-uh," Christina said. "Family business. Get out of here, Ellie, right now. And I'm going to make sure your boss knows exactly why you lost access to Griff forever."

"Bitch," Ellie spat.

Christina lunged at her, but Griff caught her before she

could make contact. "Ellie," Griff said calmly, "I suggest you leave if you ever want to work in this business again."

Laila whipped out her cell. "I'm calling the police. She's trespassing."

"Whatever!" Ellie sang before stomping off.

The three of them stood in the hallway, watching her go until the door slammed shut behind her.

Griff turned to Laila. "What was that about Dad?"

Laila's lower lip wobbled. "I'm sorry," she whispered.

"Hey, don't cry," Griff said. "This is our night to celebrate. I'm sure it's not that bad."

Laila looked to Christina and then to Griff. "Dad left me his life insurance money. A lot. Just me. I wasn't sure if I should tell you because he left you out, but you can have your share—"

"No," Griff said. "I don't need it. It's fine."

Laila bit her lip. "I'm sorry. He was a jerk. I don't know why he did that. Mom said he took out the policy ten years ago...and...I don't know what to say. I was being selfish."

"Ten years ago?" Griff asked. "That was the last time I saw him when I put out my first album."

"Maybe he knew you were going to be big," Christina said. "Maybe it was a compliment of sorts."

Laila stared at the floor. "And he knew I was just a waitress."

"But *we* know you're a songwriter," Griff said. "Water under the bridge, Laila. I'm fine with it. Now go party. This is your night to shine."

"Really?" Laila asked in a voice full of hope.

"Really," Griff said.

Laila hugged him tight and ran downstairs.

He hadn't even asked how much money it was. His heart was *always* in the right place. Christina grabbed her man and pulled him inside the bedroom, shut the door, and launched herself at him.

He caught her and they kissed passionately. Finally Griff lifted his head long enough to say, "Does this mean I'm forgiven?"

"Yes! I shouldn't have run off. I'm sorry."

He turned and pinned her against the door, kissing her again. "No, I'm sorry. You shouldn't have to be in the spot-light like that. Our relationship is private."

"Did you really mean what you said about how we're together forever even without a piece of paper saying so?"

He searched her face. "How can you even question it? Don't you know how much I love you?"

"Yes, of course I do."

"Some part of you doesn't." He kissed her tenderly. "I'm okay with that. I'll keep trying, the rest of my life if I have to, until you believe deep down that you are it for me."

Tears sprang to her eyes. "Oh, Griff."

"I'm signing over all of my money to you."

"No! Why would you do that?"

"Because I want you to have everything I have to give."

She knew money was wrapped up with love for him. He gave money with heart. He provided for his ex's brother when he was under no obligation to, contributed a sizeable donation to her brother's school music program as a peace offering, and spent his first big paycheck not on himself, but on his mother, buying her a house. She had to take a leap of faith and trust him with her own heart.

She stroked his scruffy jaw. "I don't need that. All I need is you."

His soulful hazel eyes got shiny, which made her cry.

She threw her arms around his neck and hugged him tightly. They stayed like that for a long time.

Griffin breathed a sigh of relief. He'd finally gotten through to Christina. The woman hardly ever cried, and he knew it was because she felt deep down the strength of his love.

Someone pounded on the bedroom door. "Get your ass downstairs, birthday boy! I flew in from LA for this!" It was Jake, his former bandmate and keyboard player.

"Go hang with my sister, Laila," Griffin hollered back through the door, his arms still full of Christina. "We'll be down soon."

"You have a sister?" Jake asked.

"Yes. Tell her I sent you."

"Is she hot?"

Griffin put down Christina and yanked open the door. "She's my sister. Geez, Jake."

Jake grinned, his blue eyes dancing with mischief. "Hey, old man." He hugged Griffin and pounded him on the back. They were the same age, so Griffin didn't take offense.

Christina smiled. "Look at you! Well-groomed beard, mustache, glasses. You almost look respectable."

Jake kissed her on the cheek. "I'm a high school music teacher now. Gotta look a little less badass."

"You ready to join the party?" Griffin asked Christina.

"Let's rock and roll," she replied.

He gave her a smacking kiss on the lips and headed downstairs, where the party was already in full swing. His sister had set up a nice spread of food and was busy welcoming each new arrival. Sydney and friends made an appearance and, damn, if Laila wasn't glowing as Sydney praised her performance. Most of the guests were musicians, friends he'd picked up along the years, but he was happiest to see Jake again. His other bandmate, Henry, never forgave him for breaking up the band, but Jake said he'd never been happier than teaching the next generation music.

Griffin celebrated his big-number birthday with Christina at his side like he wanted her for every birthday. Laila and Jake seemed to hit it off and chatted quite a bit off in the corner. The party went late into the night and was especially sweet for him because just as he was drifting off to sleep a new song came to him almost fully formed about soul mates. He grabbed his guitar to capture it. It was the best birthday gift he could've gotten from his muse and soul mate Christina.

Christina stretched lazily the next morning after a long makeup sex session with Griff. He'd been slow and tender in the way that rocked her body and soul. They were leaving tomorrow. She'd kind of miss this place. They had precious little vacation time with just the two of them, and it had been especially touching to see Griff with his sister.

Griff sat up, naked, and grabbed his guitar. "I wrote something new for you."

"You did? When?"

"Last night. You slept right through it."

"Let's hear it," she said, propping a pillow against the headboard and closing her eyes.

And then Griff blew her away with an incredibly emotional song about soul mates. They both had tears in their eyes when he finished.

Her throat was so tight she couldn't get a word out.

"What do you think?" he asked softly, setting his guitar down.

His tone just about killed her. His heart was sitting in her hands with that incredible song, and she didn't take that lightly. She closed the space between them, climbed into his lap and wrapped her arms and legs around him. She held his scruffy cheeks in both her hands and gazed into the hazel eyes of the man she loved heart and soul. "I think I want you to marry me."

He blinked. "Y-you do?"

"I do!" she cried.

And then they were kissing and showering each other with *I love yous*. The light of hope pushed any remaining doubts away. They were soul mates.

She was his.

He was hers.

Nothing else mattered.

EPILOGUE

Five years later…

"Okay, one more song, and then it's sleepy time," Griff said rather unconvincingly to their four-year-old twin girls.

Christina refrained from rolling her eyes as Griff launched into the girls' favorite song from a grating cartoon movie about fairies. He'd made bedtime a never-ending event with his minimum repertoire of three songs each, and she loved every minute of it. The only bad thing was when he had a gig past the girls' bedtime, because mom's voice just wouldn't do.

The girls, Willow and Sage, were enthralled, sitting up in their shared queen-size bed, looking wide awake as they joined their dad for the chorus about plucking the petals and counting them in hopes of love. They had their dad's tender, soulful side. The girls weren't identical, but they both had their dad's black hair and her blue eyes. They were the most beautiful children on the planet, if you asked her.

She and Griff had married quietly, secretly, back in New York shortly after their trip to Fieldridge. Griff had shocked the hell out of her with his own vows that spelled out his dedication to her and any children they might have. He'd given it way more thought than she had, and he'd carried through on every promise. Griff cut back on concert dates, performing only in the Northeast during the school year. Though the girls were just in preschool, he wanted to be there after school. He wanted to be *involved*. The summer was for touring, and the girls traveled everywhere with them. Griff started them on piano lessons this year, and next year they both would receive their first guitar for their fifth birthday.

The hideously saccharine song finally ended.

"More, more," the girls chanted in unison.

Griff turned to her. "You want to sing the one about the dragons?"

"Mommy's songs hurt my ears!" Willow cried.

Sage clapped her hands over her ears. "Yeah!"

"I'll tell them a story," Christina said. "But you have to lie down, eyes closed. It's getting late."

"But Daddy says we live in the city that never sleeps," Sage said. They had a two-story Manhattan apartment with two bodyguards, one for each child (at Griff's insistence). They also had a second home in Fieldridge that Laila lived in and looked after for them when they weren't there. Griff had put a recording studio in upstairs, where Laila often worked, composing original music. She'd gotten songwriting credits on Griff's last two albums.

She shot Griff a look, who merely smiled and ruffled Sage's hair. "That's what the city is for grown-ups," she said firmly, "but if kids never slept, they'd never grow. All your growing happens when you sleep."

Sage immediately closed her eyes. Willow didn't. "I don't want to grow up," she announced.

"I don't want you to grow up either," Griff said. "But you do need to sleep. Last story."

She told them their favorite story about how she and their daddy met, how they fell in love, and through music and the power of love got the ultimate gift of all—the two best children in the world. Of course, that always led to a chorus of:

"You're the best mommy in the world."

"You're the best daddy in the world."

To which they replied, "Thank you" and slowly backed out of the room while the girls launched into their usual argument with each other:

"I'm the best girl."

"No, I'm the best girl."

Which finally ended when Christina turned off the light and announced in a no-nonsense tone, "Everyone's the best. Now go to sleep."

The girls got quiet. Griff took her hand and led her downstairs. She settled on the sofa next to him and curled up against his side as he slipped an arm around her shoulders. "I'm exhausted."

Griff kissed her temple. "Let's have another one."

She flopped down in his lap, playing dead.

"No?" he asked, running his warm hand through her hair.

"I'm too old," she said.

"We'll adopt."

Her eyes flew open. "Really?" There were so many children in the world that needed a good home. They had the means and the love to provide that.

He grinned. "Really."

She sat up, suddenly energized. "We'll need to hire help."

"Then that's what we'll do."

She threw her arms around him and kissed him. Things heated up quickly right there on the sofa, which was how they ended up with their first son nine months later. Two more kids followed soon after, a boy and a girl, both adopted. Every one of them raised with music and convinced they were the best children in the world.

Laila went to work for her usual shift at Ernie's Diner that summer, looking forward to when her brother and his family came through town again. She didn't need the money from waitressing anymore, but she still worked there part time for the inspiration. It kept her grounded, reminded her of her history, and overhearing conversations and watching customer's expressions fed her artist's soul.

She'd racked up several songwriting credits as word got out about her part in Griffin's albums. She kept in touch with Jake too, from Griffin's old band, chatting over the phone about music and playing new pieces for him by Skype. They didn't live near each other, but he planned a visit next month. He'd just gotten out of a long relationship. She didn't know what that meant for her, but she held onto a little bit of hope.

And then a song came on the radio that stopped her in her tracks. It was her latest for Griffin about family, inspired by his growing family, and it was finally getting airtime.

"Here's a new one from Griffin Huntley," the DJ crooned. "Tell me if it doesn't give you *all* of the feels."

She clapped a hand over her mouth and stood frozen in place. Hearing her brother perform her music never got old. The diner quieted down and Carol came out from the kitchen to listen. Her boss and friend smiled and pointed at her, knowing her part in writing the song. Laila nodded.

And when the song finished, Carol announced, "The very talented Laila Colton will perform that song just for us Saturday seven o'clock sharp." This was not all that surprising. Every time a new song of hers hit the air, Carol wanted to celebrate with a special performance followed by a homemade chocolate cake with white iced music notes dancing across the top. Carol turned to her. "Don't worry, hon. I'll take care of everything."

Laila couldn't help but smile. "I'll be there."

And then she went back to work, secretly soaking in the community that was the beating heart of her music.

Don't miss the next book in the series, *Almost in Love,* featuring Barry and Amber, a friends-to-lovers romance!

Almost in Love

Successful entrepreneur Barry Furnukle is ready to take things to the next level with the pink-haired neighbor he adores. On advice from his ladies' man brother, Barry returns to his acting roots, where he's always universally admired. Suddenly he's got more female attention than he knows what to do with. But will his newfound popularity make him happy? Or will he channel all his sweet and sexy charm to win the woman he can't forget?

Sign up for my newsletter and never miss a new release! https://www.kyliegilmore.com/newsletter

ALSO BY KYLIE GILMORE

Unleashed Romance <<steamy romcoms with dogs!

Fetching (Book 1)

Dashing (Book 2)

Sporting (Book 3)

Toying (Book 4)

Blazing (Book 5)

Chasing (Book 6)

Daring (Book 7)

Leading (Book 8)

Racing (Book 9)

Loving (Book 10)

The Clover Park Series <<brothers who put family first!

The Opposite of Wild (Book 1)

Daisy Does It All (Book 2)

Bad Taste in Men (Book 3)

Kissing Santa (Book 4)

Restless Harmony (Book 5)

Not My Romeo (Book 6)

Rev Me Up (Book 7)

An Ambitious Engagement (Book 8)

Clutch Player (Book 9)

A Tempting Friendship (Book 10)

Clover Park Bride: Nico and Lily's Wedding

A Valentine's Day Gift (Book 11)

Maggie Meets Her Match (Book 12)

The Clover Park Charmers series <<sweet and sexy charmers!

Almost Over It (Book 1)

Almost Married (Book 2)

Almost Fate (Book 3)

Almost in Love (Book 4)

Almost Romance (Book 5)

Almost Hitched (Book 6)

Happy Endings Book Club Series <<the Campbell family and a romance book club collide!

Hidden Hollywood (Book 1)

Inviting Trouble (Book 2)

So Revealing (Book 3)

Formal Arrangement (Book 4)

Bad Boy Done Wrong (Book 5)

Mess With Me (Book 6)

Resisting Fate (Book 7)

Chance of Romance (Book 8)

Wicked Flirt (Book 9)

An Inconvenient Plan (Book 10)

A Happy Endings Wedding (Book 11)

The Rourkes Series <<swoonworthy princes and kickass princesses!

Royal Catch (Book 1)

Royal Hottie (Book 2)

Royal Darling (Book 3)

Royal Charmer (Book 4)

Royal Player (Book 5)

Royal Shark (Book 6)

Rogue Prince (Book 7)

Rogue Gentleman (Book 8)

Rogue Rascal (Book 9)

Rogue Angel (Book 10)

Rogue Devil (Book 11)

Rogue Beast (Book 12)

**Check out my website for the most up-to-date list of my books:
kyliegilmore.com/books**

ABOUT THE AUTHOR

Kylie Gilmore is the *USA Today* bestselling author of over fifty humorous contemporary romances. Her series include Unleashed Romance, the Rourkes, the Happy Endings Book Club, Clover Park, and Clover Park Charmers. With more than three million downloads of her books, readers all over the world love escaping into her hilarious feel-good romances featuring strong bonds with family, friends, and community.

Kylie lives in New York with her family, a demanding cat, and a nutso dog. When she's not writing, reading hot romance, or dutifully taking notes at writing conferences, you can find her flexing her muscles all the way to the high cabinet for her secret chocolate stash.

Sign up for Kylie's Newsletter and get a FREE book! kyliegilmore.com/newsletter

For text alerts on Kylie's new releases, text KYLIE to the number (888) 707-3025. (US only)

For more fun stuff check out Kylie's website https://www.kyliegilmore.com.

Thanks for reading *Almost Fate*. I hope you enjoyed it. Would you like to know about new releases? You can sign up for my new release email list at kyliegilmore.com/newsletter. I promise not to clog your inbox! Only new release info, sales, and some fun giveaways.

I love to hear from readers! You can find me at:
kyliegilmore.com
Facebook.com/KylieGilmoreToo
Twitter @KylieGilmoreToo

If you liked Griffin and Christina's story, please leave a review on your favorite retailer's website or Goodreads. Thank you.

Books by Shirleen Davies

Historical Western Romance Series

MacLarens of Fire Mountain

Tougher than the Rest, Book One
Faster than the Rest, Book Two
Harder than the Rest, Book Three
Stronger than the Rest, Book Four
Deadlier than the Rest, Book Five
Wilder than the Rest, Book Six

Redemption Mountain

Redemption's Edge, Book One
Wildfire Creek, Book Two
Sunrise Ridge, Book Three
Dixie Moon, Book Four
Survivor Pass, Book Five

MacLarens of Boundary Mountain

Colin's Quest, Book One,
Brodie's Gamble, Book Two, Releasing 2016

Contemporary Romance Series

MacLarens of Fire Mountain

Second Summer, Book One
Hard Landing, Book Two
One More Day, Book Three
All Your Nights, Book Four
Always Love You, Book Five
Hearts Don't Lie, Book Six
No Getting Over You, Book Seven
'Til the Sun Comes Up, Book Eight, Releasing 2016

Peregrine Bay

Reclaiming Love, Book One, A Novella
Our Kind of Love, Book Two

The best way to stay in touch is to subscribe to my newsletter. Go to

www.shirleendavies.com and subscribe in the box at the top of the right column that asks for your email. You'll be notified of new books before they are released, have chances to win great prizes, and receive other subscriber-only specials.